Diane Langford was b
England in 1963. She h
and was active in trade
Shame About the Street i

Other 90s titles

Keverne Barrett   *Unsuitable Arrangements*

Neil Bartlett   *Ready to Catch Him Should He Fall*

Suzannah Dunn   *Darker Days Than Usual*

Albyn Leah Hall   *Deliria*

James Lansbury   *Korzeniowski*

Eroica Mildmay   *Lucker and Tiffany Peel Out*

Silvia Sanza   *Alex Wants to Call it Love*

Susan Schmidt   *Winging It*

Mary Scott   *Not in Newbury and Nudists May Be Encountered*

Atima Srivastava   *Transmission*

Lynne Tillman   *Absence Makes the Heart*

Colm Tóibín   *The South*
(Winner of the 1991 *Irish Times* Aer Lingus Fiction Prize)

Margaret Wilkinson   *Ocean Avenue*

shame about the street

diane langford

This volume was published with assistance from the
Ralph Lewis Award at the University of Sussex.

Library of Congress Catalog Card Number: 93–83892

A CIP record of this book can be obtained from the
British Library on request

This is a work of fiction. Any resemblance to people
living or dead is purely coincidental

First published 1993 by
Serpent's Tail, 4 Blackstock Mews, London N4
and 401 West Broadway #1, New York, NY 10012

Set in 10½/14pt Goudy by Contour Typesetters, Southall, London
Printed in Great Britain by Cox & Wyman Ltd,
of Reading, Berkshire

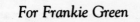
For Frankie Green

chapter 1

With a loud clattering of doors, the 8.42 from Tunbridge Wells disgorged its passengers and off they streamed, blank-faced, to hundreds of different shops and offices.

Rosemary, who enjoyed the anonymity of the crowd, regretted the moment when the sea of commuters parted and they all struck out on their own.

As always, a chauffeur-driven car hovered near the taxi-rank waiting to take her to the Ministry, a pretension she had never learned to accept and which was out of all proportion to her lowly place in the hierarchy. This posthumous favour to her long-dead father, she interpreted as unwarranted interference in her life on the part of Ministry bureaucrats who thought they knew what her father would have wanted. They were still buttering him up, hedging their bets in case his influence extended into the afterlife.

She averted her eyes from the smooth neck of the driver and forced herself to reply to small talk about traffic and weather.

"There's a flap on about a leak," the woman said suddenly. Rosemary was miles away, thinking how pleasant it would be to live alone.

"Even us drivers are being questioned," the woman persisted as the limousine paused at a pedestrian crossing. Rosemary felt she was being critically scrutinized in the rear view mirror and she had to break the driver's intrusive stare by peering stupidly out of the window as the car moved off. As she did so a woman with a baby in her arms stepped off the pavement, pressed the child's dirty face against the window and held out her hand in a begging gesture which reminded Rosemary of school holidays in New Delhi when crowds ran alongside her father's limousine, hands outstretched, shouting "Memsahib, Memsahib . . ." And it was hot. People milling by wore cotton trousers, skirts and canvas shoes.

Rosemary's irritation showed when she addressed the driver.

"What secrets could you possibly know?" she said in her tight memsahib voice.

"We all signed the Official Secrets Act, same as you," the woman retorted sharply.

This was of no possible concern to Rosemary. She was a minor administrator, not a policymaker, and was conscious a sinecure had been created for her as part of an exercise in empire-building by someone higher up the ladder to increase the number of rungs.

She performed her work efficiently, such as it was, routine stuff, leaving a large part of the day free to listen to soaps on her personal radio and do crossword puzzles. Her secretary knew to deflect visitors and phone calls when the Archers were going through a critical period, as the time when they all feared Kenton may have been lost at sea.

She nestled into the soft cream leather, took out *The Daily Telegraph* and ran her eye down the crossword clues. They were nearing Whitehall.

"Poor old Rosie, what a devil of a journey," her mother told neighbours. "And she doesn't have to work, she knows that." And Rosemary always felt a twinge of guilt but mostly relief as she made her Monday to Friday escape from the old lady's incessant chatter.

Her mother's life had been more interesting than her own but that wasn't Rosemary's fault. She had been packed off to a succession of boarding schools while Celeste, her mother, had lived it up in colonial splendour in the twilight of the Raj.

And when tales of the British in India were made into a television series, Celeste blatantly identified with the English rose liberal heroine, and would not be budged from in front of the television sceen.

"See that darling? Daddy and I were there, and the Mountbattens came to tea. Every year, between June and August, I went up the hill station at Simla . . . daddy couldn't always get away . . ."

Whenever Celeste embarked on yet another tale of the Raj, Rosemary knew it would lead to the same old theme.

"You should get out more. Make something of your life. Leap out of the rut! You're not bad looking in a tall, striding, Glenda Jacksonish sort of way. Women like you were called 'handsome' in my day. I don't know the current argot . . ."

"I'm quite happy as I am, thank you," Rosemary answered crisply.

Once though, her mother hinted at something unspeakable that went on in all-girl schools, to which Rosemary simply replied calmly, "What would you know about it?"

"Times have changed, darling. No-one minds that sort of thing nowadays, In fact, it's rather fashionable," Celeste cackled wickedly.

"You don't know what you're talking about."

Her furious look quelled the torrent of words. Then a few minutes later, like a naughty child who can keep quiet only for a few minutes at a time, Celeste renewed the endless stream.

Rosemary despised all frivolity, gossipy intrusion, probing, poking and provoking. All she wanted was to be left alone. She thrived on her inner existence and could have sat all day thinking about nothing in particular, re-running pleasant times on the virtual reality inside her head. Old conversations, daydreaming of the different twists and turns her life might have taken if only . . .

This was a contented, not regretful pastime. She did not envy her mother's former grand lifestyle and avid socializing. Now the old lady was so dependent upon her, Rosemary had grown detached. All that ostentation had been so much hot air and completely out of tune with her father's ascetic nature. When Nehru's midnight hour struck, Celeste and all her cronies and hangers-on had to scramble out of India in unseemly haste, back to mundanity.

As she alighted from the car the driver gave Rosemary a long, penetrating look which caused her to flush to the roots of her hair. Was she experiencing an early menopause?

Mary screwed up a paper napkin and wiped her face. The canteen was hot and crowded. Other women at her table flipped the pages of a mail order catalogue and blew smoke across the table as if their lives depended on it.

She looked at her watch. Seven thirty-five.

"All right, babe?" her friend Reen asked, nudging her foot under the table. Reen had a nose for trouble.

"Yeah, just a bit tired."

At 8 am the day shift — printworkers and journalists — would come on duty and begin filling the bins and ashtrays, smearing dirty fingermarks on walls, sneezing on mirrors, and soiling the lavatories all over again. Mary was full of contempt for the people whose shit she had to clean up.

She edged her feet closer together, clamping her shopping bag between her thighs. Ever since a few packets of scampi and frozen steaks went missing from the freezer, security men searched the bags of canteen workers and cleaners as they left the building.

"You look poorly," Reen said.

"Just knackered . . ." If only she could think of something bright to throw her friend off the scent. "Why does it say Mr Chippy?' she said, pointing to the logo on the crumpled paper napkin. It really puzzled her. Mr Chippy was a company that ran a well-known chain of motorway services.

"Same firm," said Reen knowledgeably. "Same outfit runs the motorway caffs. That's why this lot aren't in the union. All contract workers. You think us cleaners are paid crap? You wouldn't believe what they're getting an hour." She was on her soap-box again.

All the Mr Chippy workers were black people. The cleaners were all white and belonged to the local branch of a print union.

"Closed shop apartheid," Reen muttered sourly.

Nell, the union rep, slapped down her magazine. Mary flinched as the bad vibes passed between the two women. They were always having rows about the union. According to Nell the closed shop had only existed to ensure 100 per cent union membership. Reen saw it as a way of keeping women down and black people out. Mary felt awkward, caught between the two Queen Bees. Nell had the power and authority of her post as the women's supervisor and in her other role as Mother of the Chapel. She controlled their lives at work by drawing up rosters favouring friends, and penalizing those out of favour by giving them the shittiest jobs. She was also responsible for allocating overtime which meant she could even get you a couple of hours extra pay here and there. Mary didn't want to tread on her toes. To make matters worse, she was a neighbour, she lived in the same block, one floor up.

"When Fleet Street was in its heyday everyone was in a union," Nell said, challenging Reen. "Now we've got private security firms, Mr Chippy, and any odds and sods the guv'nors want to bring in. None of them in the union. It's ruined the atmosphere. You could hold your head up in the print. Not any more."

Mary hoped she wasn't going to go on about her old man, Jack, who was ashamed to tell his mates in the pub what he used to do before he became a full-time union official: women's work!

"Pissing little keyboards any typist off the street could operate," Nell went on as the other women looked at each other wearily. Most of them had a husband, father or brother in the trade.

"A few years back they'd never of tried on this searching business, would they Reen?'

"No way!" Reen had to agree.

"They'd never of got away with it," Nell confirmed, mashing out her cigarette. "Bloody paper would of shut down, just like that."

When Mary asked what Mother of the Chapel meant, Nell said it was adapted from Father of the Chapel and was left over from the days of monks printing Bibles. But, as usual, Reen disagreed. She said it was from when the first printers used to meet in chapels to form secret unions. If caught they were thrown in jail, deported, or even hanged.

Mary's husband was a union man. It was through him the Union head office sent her for the job. Nell, who had the power of hiring and firing, took her on and showed her the ropes. It took Mary a while to grasp the fact that although Nell was the women's supervisor, appointed by the management, she was also their union rep. It bothered her so much that she put her foot right in it by inquiring naively. "How can you do both?" That feckin' cow, Nell, hardly spoke to her for a week.

By now, Mary realized the union were never going to do fuck-all about the searches because she'd already had words with Nell, who, for another few weeks after that had been prickly with her. "It is bloody awkward, them being neighbours," she thought again.

"It's the ones doing the thieving who make things bad for everyone else," was Nell's final word. "It's nothing to do with the union."

And she showed new recruits around as if she'd built the effing place with her own hands.

"It's a listed building," she said proudly, pointing out the lovely brass lights in the entrance hall and the beautiful marble staircase.

But once you got past the lobby and the fairyland staircase ended, what a tip! Mary couldn't believe it the night she started. She'd never seen anything like it. Paper everywhere. Balls of it, bails of it, strips of it, reels of it.

The women had to wheel it away in carts, take it down the back way in the goods lift and dump it in Shoe Lane.

All night long the teleprinters clattered, spewing out long ribbons of ticker tape. The third floor marked EDITORIAL was the worst. The women worked in teams and took turns cleaning different floors each night. The sixth floor was most popular because it was least messy and you could sit down, have a fag and watch *Goodmorning Britain* on the director's telly, pee in his private bathroom, or even take a shower surrounded by black tiles and mirrors.

Then, over the last few months, the piles of paper began getting smaller and the women calculated that jobs would be lost.

As MoC, Nell assumed an air of self-importance that Mary learned to distrust and dislike. Reen felt the same, she was sure. Mary was waiting for an opportunity to have a good talk about it but it wasn't easy to catch Reen on her own. After all, it was Nell who made up the rotas and decided who worked with who.

At ten to eight the women stubbed out their fags and prepared to leave.

"Coming Mary?" called Reen. They usually got the 63 down the Elephant together.

"Haven't finished me tea," Mary mumbled and kept sitting. It was horrible not being able to say anything to Reen who gave her a funny look and walked off with the others.

It was an unwritten rule that the cleaners got out of the canteen before the day workers came in. And now they were drifting in with ill-humoured faces, lining up for toast and coffee before starting work.

Mary felt them scowling at her, bad-vibing her, but there was no way she could move from where she was stuck, stranded like a nymph on a feckin' rock.

Madeline was by the lift, staring intently at the glowing lights that indicated the floor numbers. Any moment now the editor-in-chief would enter the lobby, greet the front-hall attendants like old mates, getting their names all wrong and making a complete dickhead of himself as usual. She wanted the lift to arrive before he did. Trapped in a confined space with Colin Shadbolt was not her idea of a fun way to start the day.

But he walked right on by, ignoring her, to the directors' lift where he made a great display of using a special key, then he disappeared into the plush, smoked glass box.

What a turn-up! Since when had the directors given Shadbolt a key? She stabbed the lift button impatiently; only ten minutes to go before her shift started and she needed her breakfast.

It was stifling in the canteen and there was a long queue. One of the revolting young night subs mooched in and stood behind her with his hands bunched in his pockets.

"Oh, brill, it's you," he said insincerely.

"Don't call me brill," she snapped.

He suppressed a yawn. "Another fuckin' DC10 down last night," he whined, "we were up all fuckin' night. Didn't get our heads down once."

"Well you *are* here to work," she replied sharply, preoccupied with her breakfast order. Bacon and egg or sausage and egg?

"Lots of brats on board, fuckin' school team. Came down in the fuckin' sea . . ."

Madeline clucked with irritation.

"Here, you get this shit," he said, suddenly pulling a scrap of steno paper out of his pocket. "It's the breakfast list." He thrust it into her hands and moved briskly away.

"You little bastard," she shouted after him just as a bunch of cleaning women walked by.

"Orright love?" called out the one whose name she thought was Nell. They were all Nellies, Daisies or Rosies. Maybe in the year 2020 there'll be armies of cleaning women called Tracy, Sharon and Kylie, Madeline speculated.

"Yeah, so so," she answered. It was her turn in the queue and the clock's hands were pointing to eight. "Four double sausage and egg, two eggs and bacon and six coffees to take out, ta," she read the list to the perspiring woman behind the counter.

One of the cleaners, the little Irish one, was still sitting in the corner. As Madeline looked over the woman beckoned. Madeline squinted and the woman signalled again. How bizarre!

Maybe she'd better sit down and have her fix of black coffee before she started feeling faint. If she didn't drink her mug of coffee and consume her bacon and egg sarnie before she started work, she couldn't make it through the day. And now that she'd been promoted to breakfast monitor, she had all the time in the world.

"Hi," she said, sitting down. "You're Mary aren't you?' The poor girl looked awful, tired and harassed, with purple welts under her eyes, prominent under the harsh strip lighting.

"I want to ask a favour," Mary started nervously. "Just say if you think it's a liberty . . . well, it is a liberty . . ."

"What is it?" Madeline asked, impatiently ripping the grease-sodden wrapper off a sandwich.

Mary leaned across the table, "Did you know we get searched as we leave?"

"I heard something about it. Bloody outrageous!"

Madeline was feeling better already.

"Well, I don't want to get searched today. I haven't pinched no steaks or nothing. Not that I blame those who do. Not on what they earn."

"What is it then?" Madeline asked suspiciously.

"It's sort of union stuff," Mary answered.

"I thought Nellie was your MoC," Madeline said.

"She is, but this is sort of unofficial, know what I mean?"

Madeline sucked at her coffee. It was as if the woman was testing her. "I don't see where I fit in," she said cagily.

"Well, if I left me carrier bag in the ladies' bog, you could collect it and take it without being searched."

Madeline contemplated the heap of congealed grease piled on the table in front of her. She put her hand round one of the styrofoam coffee cups. It was nicely tepid.

Mary was looking at her appealingly.

"OK," Madeline said, "you're on, just as soon as I've delivered this lot to those bastards upstairs. Give me fifteen minutes. I'll be in the betting shop over the road." She always felt decisive and confident after her bacon and egg sarnie. It hits the bloodstream instantly. The trick is to eat it hot and fast.

chapter 2

Miss Alexander looked over her half-glasses and murmured in her irritating, twee fashion:

"His nibs wants to see you."

"Hmmm . . . first things first . . ."

Rosemary strode into her office. Her secretary fluttered along at her heels, took her oatmeal linen jacket with an ingratiating smirk and hung it with devotion on the antique coat rack. Rosemary went through her usual routine of signing on to the computer terminal on her desk using a password known only to herself, the systems people, and Sir Gregory. However, she doubted whether Sir Gregory would have the slightest inkling how to switch the machine on.

The terminal flashed "You have no messages" across its green face. It was the same every morning.

With an indifferent expression, Rosemary keyed in a code which enabled her to read the list of staff attached to her department.

The woman's name was Lorraine Frances Leonard, aged thirty-five, previously employed as a driver by the Ministry of Defence, unmarried, next-of-kin an aunt in Scotland. Rosemary remembered the woman's attractive, throaty laugh and the confident way she manoeuvred the big car. Her reverie was interrupted when Miss Alexander appeared with a pot of tea and a plate of dry biscuits.

"He did ask to see you as soon as you arrived," she said fussily, "but I thought you might need a little pick-me-up first."

Rosemary frowned at her secretary's conspiratorial manner. She hated it when people did not behave the way they were supposed to. What was going on?

Sir Gregory sat behind his desk in a formal pose, dressed in the usual immaculate dark suit, his nut-brown pate visible between puffs of blow-dried silver fluff. His pale eyes appeared even paler against the artificially tanned skin. It was like looking through him and seeing daylight out the other side.

He sat dead centre, perfectly still, with the tips of his fingers lightly touching. There was a manilla folder placed symmetrically in front of him. The black and white diamond-pattern flooring was soft to walk on, made of rubberized fibre glass. Beams of sunlight fell on the honey-coloured panelling in the huge office. There were pretty flower boxes on the sills of the enormous windows. Cherubs with round bellies and full lips intertwined in the cornices.

"Sit down will you, Miss um . . . Rosemary . . ."

In his presence, she felt the same old awkwardness at being expected to make responses to his monotonous monologues. If she kept quiet he might infer lack of interest. If she said too much, she might appear pushy.

As she seated herself, a far-off door opened and in glided Sir Gregory's secretary. Without a word, he went behind a lacquered screen in the corner, switched on a machine and went out silently.

"I hope your mother's well." Sir Gregory said, lowering his eyes to the file.

"Yes, she is, very well thank you."

After previous audiences, Rosemary had come away mystified. No apparent purpose had been served by such interviews. She knew he hardly ever spent time at the Ministry and was more often to be found in one of his clubs. This must be one of his token appearances. Was his inquiry as to her mother's health a trick question?

She found it difficult to focus on what he was saying. He spoke in the same stilted, toneless voice he used when dictating letters.

"The fact is, there has been a serious breach of confidence, a leak, emanating from this office," he went on. What was this to do with her? She couldn't understand why he was telling her this.

He turned the folder to face her and flicked it open with his thumb. Neatly pinned inside were the front pages of half a dozen tabloid newspapers. Her eyes skimmed a jumble of words she could not grasp. The headlines palpitated in front of her eyes. Perverts. Leak. Outlaw. Queers. As Sir Gregory's voice droned on she strained to listen and comprehend. ". . . a formality . . . in your own interest . . . leave of absence on full pay . . ."

Was she being accused? Of what? How could it be the thing she was beginning to think it was? The thing she had always dreaded. Had Sir Gregory read her mind, divined the secret longings which tormented her in moments of weakness?

"Naturally, we will be sorry to let you go. But you do appreciate, this puts the department in an extremely invidious position. Your family links, the respect in which everyone holds your late father . . ."

Years of suppressed, intimate thoughts and desires imploded and cascaded inside her head. Things no-one knew, no-one could know because she had never told. Sitting, with her feet planted squarely in front of her, hands folded neatly on her lap, she felt as if she was dropping through the floor.

"I don't understand! What's any of this got to do with me?" she managed to croak. Behind the screen a tape wound on inexorably, whirring slightly. So, their conversation was being taped. Hence his measured speech.

How dare he speak of her father! This man who claimed to be her father's friend, whose eyes were hard as pebbles, who had a foul, diseased mind. Thank God her father was dead and out of it.

Everything looked different. As if her whole life had been leading inevitably to this moment of complete humiliation: as if her private parts had been spread over the front page of every newspaper in the land, arriving on people's doormats to be pored over at the breakfast table.

Her mind was in utter confusion. What did it mean? Why her? How could anyone possibly know what went on inside her head?

It was a long way back to her office and with each step an effort of will was required to stop her from flying to pieces.

Miss Alexander sat erect at her post, biting her lip and blinking back tears.

"A representative from the civil servants' union is waiting to see you," she informed Rosemary nervously.

"I don't want to see them. I wouldn't ask them for help if they were the last people on earth."

All she had to be proud of was her absolute, profound respectability. She had done nothing wrong.

Celeste took a strange delight in the situation, devouring the tabloids like a scavenger bird.

When Rosemary's name was romantically linked to a famous woman newsreader with a million pound job, Celeste's guffaws and snorts dislodged her spectacles.

There in the paper was a photograph of the newsreader in a fashionable restaurant, leaning across the table towards a companion whose face was in shadow. Their hands were touching. A white circle was superimposed around the head of the other woman whose face was invisible.

"Lusty Lesley and Mole Girl Dine at L'Escargot" read the caption.

"Isn't it wonderful!" hooted Celeste. "It's like a spot-the-ball competition. One cannot even make out the gender of the person who's supposed to be you, darling! One should complain. I would if I were you. Why didn't they use one of those zoom lenses?"

"Because if they did, everyone could see it isn't me, you silly old goat. Don't you know what they're calling me?" Rosemary shouted. "A filthy lesbian!" Once the word flew out and hung in the air, Rosemary half expected to be struck down by a bolt of lightning, but nothing happened.

Celeste read on, oblivious to the trauma Rosemary was suffering.

" 'A denial has been issued.' Do you hear that? Listen to this: 'The Minister was using his Tandy to run a few ideas up the flagpole, the result was accessed by an unauthorised user, a leak occurred. A civil servant in the Minister's private office has been suspended on full pay while an internal investigation is carried out.' They haven't mentioned your name.

Celeste continued: "'There are no firm plans to re-criminalize homosexuality in this parliament, although we are very cognisant of the strong public demand to do so,' a Whitehall spokesperson said."

"What a lot of poppycock! There's no such demand," Celeste snorted.

"Keep away from the window," Rosemary ordered her mother. But Celeste had developed a strange rapport with the band of reporters encamped on the verge opposite their house. She waved to them like the late, dear Queen Mother and dressed up especially to show herself to the press.

"We've got to keep standards up," she quipped, preening herself before the window.

She adored their efforts to trick their way into the house.

"You silly boy. Telegrams were abolished long ago," she trilled through the letter-box to Chalky White of the *Mirror*, who had obtained an obsolete uniform from an army surplus store.

chapter 3

Madeline bounded up the stairs two at a time, then found she needn't have knocked herself out. There was a queue by the entrance to Kitty's; mostly baby dykes with fresh pink faces and slickered hair.

Madeline hated queues and didn't like baby dykes much either. She glared at them and they stared back insolently, taking for granted everything women of her generation had fought for.

Leaving the cinema once, after crying her eyes out over *The Loudest Whisper* for the tenth time she heard one of them say arrogantly: "Oh God, wasn't Shirley Maclaine a wimp? You wouldn't catch *me* topping myself . . ." Before she could go further, Maddy had her by the collar.

"Haven't you got any sense of history, you snit-faced little shit!"

She was pent-up now, ready to respond if one of them tried to jump the queue. She knew Carol would fill in the time getting pissed if she was kept waiting.

The grizzle-headed woman on the door Maddy remembered well from Gateways days. She counted out the change painstakingly, fingering the bottom of a shoebox for the right coins. Every woman was stamped on the back of the hand with indelible ink. It was cheaper than issuing tickets and more fun.

Madeline's patience was wearing thin. She was bursting with wanting to tell Carol about her weird day at work.

Carol was sat near the bar, half-way through a pint of draught Guinness.

"Hi" called Madeline and waved as she saw her girlfriend move the jacket she'd used to keep the seat next to her vacant. She lip-read "Hullo sweetheart" as the house music suddenly blared. Carol had come straight from the hairdresser and wasn't happy with the result, Maddy divined, as Carol pointed to her head. "Isn't it a mess?" she yelled. "Cost me a bloody fortune, and when I queried the bill they said 'Judi Dench comes here'. I said 'who's Judi Dench?' and they said 'that's her dog tied up outside', so I said 'I don't give a fuck if Chairman Mao comes in here . . .'"

"I'll bet that floored them," Madeline shouted, then put her mouth next to Carol's ear, "You're still the best-looking woman in the room."

She looked around the long, rectangular bar as if to confirm it and spotted two of her own ex-lovers and three of Carol's.

"Have you seen who's here? Plastic Face and the Fat Fiddler!" Carol mouthed.

Maddy and Carol had silly names for each other's exes and Maddy was beginning to think the joke was wearing thin. Friends had complained it wasn't sisterly. Maddy didn't worry too much about the sisterhood stuff, but she speculated about what name Carol would invent for her if they split up.

"I'm going to get a drink," she said.

"Good. Get me a whisky chaser," said Carol.

Maddy had to lead with her shoulder to get through the crowd round the bar. Bloody hell! There was a man doing the drinks! Kitty's was an extension of the pub downstairs and he was one of their regular barmen. To give him his due the poor bastard looked suitably harassed and shamefaced.

Just as she was ordering, Maddy spotted one of the organizers of the weekly Kitty's Club nights, a veteran of Gay Liberation who used to work for the Beeb, Esme Evans.

Esme's hair dazzled whiter than white and her face was golden brown from lying under a sun lamp and frequent holidays to Lesbos. Her eyes were brilliant blue and her voice ever so posh. All in all, Maddy found her wickedly attractive. There was something in those sonorous Roedean tones that Maddy's petit-bourgeois inclinations found a great turn-on. After all, in her own way, Esme was a revolutionary. She'd founded a magazine for lesbians, set up discussion groups, bar nights, and even organized clubs for dykes in the sticks. Her newsletter advertised the services of a lesbian artist who, for an enormous fee, would render your loved-one's likeness in oils. "But would the paint have time to dry?" Maddy laughed wryly when she read it.

Esme jostled women out of the way imperiously and claimed a position in front of the bar. All eyes were on her as she ceremoniously placed a shiny brass bell with a button top on the table in front of her. When she raised her hand, the music stopped instantly. Esme pinged on the bell even though she already had their undivided attention.

"As you know," she drawled in her gorgeous BBC voice, "Kitty's Club is a lot more than simply a place where women drop in for a drink and meet their friends. We also aim to educate and entertain. So it was with great regret that I have to tell you that due to unforeseen personal difficulties, ("That means they've split up" whispered those in the know) . . . as I was saying . . . due to unforeseen circumstances the Dora Russell dance duo will not be with us tonight." She paused as a disappointed groan ran round the room. "And so," she looked over the sexy granny glasses which she wore expressly for the purpose of looking over, "and so, myself and Lorraine — or Rainey as she likes to be called . . ." She indicated an ash blonde in a white blouse and what Maddy guessed was some kind of uniform. There was a cap on the seat beside her made out of the same charcoal material as the skirt. The sight of it stirred something in Maddy's memory.

Rainey looked round and acknowledged the crowd with a self-assured smile which disappeared when Esme continued: "Rainey and I will provide an alternative entertainment, and I have to tell you Lorraine has been *so* nervous about this that she told me on the way here she was wetting her knickers."

"I did not," Rainey hissed, scarlet-faced.

"Oh?" Esme exclaimed with surprise. She raised her voice and boomed: "Did you hear that at the back? Lorraine's knickers are not, repeat *not* wet!"

Lorraine continued to look murderous as Esme explained further. "We are going to do some role-play to show you how to chat up a woman in a bar." They chatted stiltedly but loudly so everyone could hear. Then Esme said: "Now we want you to practise with the woman sitting on your right. Make sure you are not sitting next to anyone you know."

Everyone milled about self-consciously, shuffling themselves into a formation so that they were all sitting next to a stranger. Maddy noticed Carol make a bee-line for Rainey while she herself stayed where she was and let them all move round her. Now she was next to one of the baby dykes.

"What do you do for a living?" the kid asked.

"I work in Fleet Street," Maddy replied, watching Carol chatting up Rainey.

"Oh, what's that like?"

"A shit and sugar experience," Maddy said, "more shit than sugar to be quite frank."

The kid didn't have much of a line. And not much dress sense either, dungarees over a white tee-shirt with short flaring arms, and more badges on her chest than Colin Powell.

Maddy pointed to one she couldn't read without her glasses: "What does that say?"

"Support women musicians," the kid answered, sticking out her chest.

"Yeah, I supported one for four years and the bitch ran off with an opera singer," Maddy sneered, glaring at her ex but quickly switching her attention back to Carol and Rainey. They were really hitting it off, talking animatedly and laughing a lot.

Esme came to the rescue. Ping! went the bell.

chapter 4

Mary grabbed the empty front seat on top of the bus where you could spread yourself out and have a cigarette without any aggro. Most of the other traffic was heading into the city, and she was going south of the river, so the bus was moving along at a fair old clip. She was still mystified by her own strange behaviour that morning and was trying to work it out. The cigarette helped her concentrate.

Polishing the boardroom, she had found a leather-bound, spiral folder on the seat of a chair pushed under the directors' long conference table. She picked it up and at the same time noticed a gap like a missing tooth in a glass-fronted bookcase. And when she attempted to return the file to the space the sliding door refused to move. The case was locked.

Instead of putting the file back where she had found it, she peeked inside and began skimming the contents. Reen would like to see this, she thought. Acting on impulse, she put it in a black plastic sack as if it were part of the litter. Holding her breath, she switched the file from the rubbish sack into her shopping bag just before joining the other cleaners in the canteen.

It was lucky that journalist woman had come in just then. But she had taken forever to pick up the bag and bring it to the betting shop. Then she made a posy drama out of it, making herself out a heroine. Security men parading outside the bog . . . that was crap! The searches were always done in the lobby.

Mary's nerves gradually settled down. She was home free and it felt better than nicking a few lamb chops. She had succeeded in making off with a piece of the bosses' paraphernalia. It showed they weren't invincible. They had a weak spot, even if it was tiny, like a microscopic blemish in a johnny bag. That's all it took.

When she got in, Terry was sitting at the kitchen table hunched over his *Sporting World* as usual.

"Jeez, you're tense," she said, "look at those shoulders!"

"I'm late for work," he said, without looking up.

"Were you waiting for your mummy to come and make your brekky?" she said in a provocative baby voice.

The kids were picking at their cornflakes, still in their pyjamas; the girls' knotted pigtails trailed in the milky sludge.

Mary plonked her carrier bags by the sink and reached for the frying pan.

"Hurry up and get dressed, you kids," she yelled, "or you'll be late for school."

After the kids had gone Terry, who would never go out without his cooked breakfast, sullenly cleaned his plate with a lump of bread and left for work. Mary took the file and hid it in the drawer where she kept her sanny towels and tampons. He would never dare look there: he was scared of stuff like that.

Then she crawled into bed to enjoy the best part of the day, crashing out, going completely unconscious for hours until the kids came home.

But what seemed like only minutes later, her eyes were being poked out. The kids were jumping on the bed screaming. Ice-cream! Ice-cream! And she could hear the jangling hurdy-gurdy noise of the ice-cream cart down in the square.

"Take some money from my little black purse," she mumbled,

buying herself a few extra minutes peace, then fell back on the pillows exhausted.

She never thought about whether she was happy or not. Thoughts like that drove people nuts. When she tried to imagine a different kind of life, nothing came to mind except a funny kind of loneliness. If she wasn't married to Terry, didn't have the kids, her job and friends at work, what would there be? It was like looking into a deep well and sometimes just before drifting off to sleep she had a falling sensation and knew she'd wake up with a headache. So if the stairs had been hosed down and didn't stink of piss, or the lift was working or the petunias in her window box were looking perky in the sunshine, there was a moment of contentment so fleeting that it slipped away before she could pin it down. The harder she tried to hang on to such moments, the more elusive they became.

Jeez, it was hot. Better get up, have a shower, tidy the place, and make dinner. Maybe they'd go out for a beer later. She knew that when Terry came home he would be in his strong, silent mode. He would stretch out in front of the box and watch the evening news. Since he'd been elected chairman of the union branch he watched every evening. Maybe he thinks he is going to see his ugly mug on the box, Mary curled her lip as she imagined Terry's fantasy: "Trade union leader out-foxes newspaper baron in history-making negotiations."

She moved around the kitchen like an automaton, opening cupboards, going to the refrigerator; all the while chatting to Reen. Since childhood she had invented imaginary friends; the perfect companion for every shared intimacy. Inside her head she carried on long conversations with them, making up their replies. It was like playing yourself at draughts. In that way she found a sort of privacy combined with companionship. It had become a habit, except that, nowadays, Reen embodied the old, imagined companions and supplanted them. All Mary's private thoughts were directed to *her*. Sometimes, when she was actually with Reen, she got confused between the imaginary conversations and the real ones.

She rolled pizza dough into floury balls and palmed them flat on the kitchen table. Tonight she was going to make something *she* fancied and to hell with Terry and the kids. She knew what would happen. He would act hurt, pick off all the black olives and put them on the side of his plate without saying anything. The kids would whine, demand chips, then scoff the lot.

Everything went as she predicted and they were still eating and complaining when the doorbell rang. Both kids jumped up from the table and rushed down the hall pummelling each other to get to the door first.

"Who is it, who is it?" the boy yelled through the letter-box as the girl tore at his jumper.

"Stop it!" Mary screamed.

Nell was standing on the doorstep made up to the nines in a floral jacket with enormous shoulder pads and a tight-fitting black dress. A wide elasticated belt emphasized her fibroid-swollen belly.

Her weasel-faced husband, Jack, hovered behind her.

Mary opened the door wider. "Come on in."

Nell's fixed smile telegraphed her intention to enjoy herself. There was a time for work and a time for play. She was dowsed in Estée Lauder, had a good figure for her age and, but for a smoker's cough, was fit as a fiddle.

"It's me birthday," she exclaimed, then laughed. "All dressed up with nowhere to go."

"Oh God, Nell, sorry, I forgot," Mary said. "We're not quite ready." She took them into the tiny front room.

Their flats were identical except Nell's, on the landing above, was always tidy. Their kids had grown up and gone away. Then the council moved them from their house in Camberwell into a one bedroom flat and Nell told Mary she could never get used to not having a garden. She could quite happily have gone on living in the four bedroom house, just the two of them, without any qualm of conscience. Jack, though, because of his ambitions, felt obliged to tell the housing department. "The whole purpose of getting on the council is to get you and yours a decent place to live," Nell complained. "What's it all about, if not that?"

Now an Asian family was living at Number 83, and she told Mary that's what got her hackles up more than anything. Mary hated that kind of talk but she kept her mouth shut.

Apparently, Nell sometimes went back to see the woman over the road, just to keep an eye on the old street, and everything had changed. She also whinged a lot about her and Jack not having a telly like normal people. She said Jack did simple crossword puzzles and read western comics instead. And he didn't trust banks so he kept all his money in a metal box in the freezer. Mean as a shithouse rat, more like, Mary thought. Not that she could give a monkey's.

She was tired and had lost the urge to go out.

Terry was slouched over the kitchen table without making any effort to clear the dinner things away. She elbowed him in the ribs to get him to move.

"Go in there and get them a drink," she ordered, banging glasses on the table. Lazily, he got up and took three cans out of the refrigerator.

Mary stacked the dirty dishes in the oven and put a tea towel over the window of the oven door in case Nell came into the kitchen. She didn't give a toss what Nell thought but she didn't like the idea of being discussed by the women at work. "You know what her mouth's like," she told Reen in her head.

Upstairs, she rifled through her jumpers, throwing one on the floor because of a stain, another which ponged under the armpits, and a third with a hole in the elbow.

"I haven't got a thing to wear," she moaned, as it suddenly struck her that she didn't have any clothes suitable for the heat. "Everything's in the wash or far too warm. Nearly all my effing clothes are too hot for this weather."

Jesus, Mary and Joseph, what was she going to wear? A pink shirt deemed too pansy lay discarded at the bottom of Terry's half of the wardrobe, still in its perspex box. She took out the pins and cardboard and pulled it over her head. Black cotton tights, her hair tied up with a bright green scarf and a leather belt yanked in to its last notch and she was ready to boogie. When she stuck in a pair of black and silver earrings, she didn't look bad. She pulled a lock of dark, frizzy hair from under the scarf.

God, she was tired. She couldn't remember sleeping that day, just flopping into bed then being forced awake by the kids. She applied red lipstick and did some fancy work with an eyeliner before squeezing her feet into a pair of slingbacks.

The kids were still fighting and yelling. She shoved them into their room and shut the door. By the time she got downstairs, Nell was in full flood, still going on about losing her garden. Terry stared morosely into his beer, looking like an American bald eagle, with his sunken eyes, crooked neck and drooping beak.

"Oh, very, very trendy," Nell observed when Mary entered in her makeshift outfit.

Trust bloody Nell to dress up like a feckin' Christmas tree just to go to the pub. It wasn't even a proper pub. Just a bar in the community centre. Low ceiling so the smoke grew intense. Special low lighting over the pool tables.

Their row of flats was on concrete stilts with a car park underneath and a parade of shops on the ground level. Everything you could possibly need: Fag shop, offie, mini-market, unisex hair salon, betting shop. Over the road was a school, hospital and undertaker.

The walls along the walkway were daubed with the usual graffiti: KILL IRA SCUM and I PUT MY COCK UP YOUR SISTER'S ARSE. "Charming I'm sure," Nell commented as they clattered along in their too-high heels.

Whenever Mary had a drink and was tired, there was liable to be trouble. As soon as she walked in the place she knew it was on the cards. A phoney Irish band was playing "Galway Bay". Her favourite hate. It made her seasick. But she was determined not to show herself up in front of Nell.

The men got in pints, a G&T for Nell and whiskey for Mary. "You can't beat a John Jameson with a beer chaser," she told Nell and it was God's truth, as far as she was concerned.

She and Nell took turns tottering up for more drinks, while Terry and Jack ignored them. Nell tried to dance with a man standing at the bar and touched his thighs, but he turned a glazed expression on her and was incapable of cutting adrift from the support of the bar rail.

"I saw that!" Mary shrieked and they laughed and laughed till Terry noticed and shouted over: "No more for you. You're over the top . . . You're pissed."

Mary grabbed him by the shoulder. "Don't speak to me like that!"

"Get home and see to those poor little bastards," he shouted. And Nell put her hand on Mary's arm. "Come on love, are you working tomorrow?" Mary shook her head and allowed herself to be dragged along, muttering, "don't friggin' patronize me, I just don't need it, I'm not feckin' drunk."

The usual room above the snooker club was booked, so they had to use the staff canteen for the meeting. Nell was in the chair, chain-smoking and shuffling papers. The women sat in rows, waiting for the men from head office to arrive.

Mary checked her watch. She hoped it wouldn't be Terry. It was. The two men marched in self-consciously, up to the table where Nell was sitting. Only Nell knew Terry was Mary's husband and Mary gave no flicker of recognition. He didn't look at her. They'd had a massive row that morning.

He leant across Nell to speak to his colleague. "You chair the meeting Bob, OK?" They nodded and winked at each other. Nell glared and stubbed out her cigarette. "No way, I'm chairing this meeting!"

Mary squirmed. Angry words were being exchanged. Nell looked fierce. She stood up and rapped the table.

"Listen everyone," she exclaimed, "a difference of opinion has come up as to who is going to chair this meeting." She paused and looked round the room, felt inside her handbag and produced a fresh packet of cigarettes, lit one up and blew columns of smoke out of her nostrils before going on.

"The question is, who should chair this meeting. Me, or this gent from head office who is an unknown quantity to us?"

The women muttered: "That's not fair, that's out of order . . ."

"So," Nell continued, "I suggest we settle this like we settle everything in this chapel. That is, the old-fashioned way — by a show of hands."

"Tell 'im Nellie," the women called out, whistling and stamping as Nell sat down triumphantly.

Terry looked sheepish. "There's no need for that," he said. "You can carry on."

"Thank you so much. That's very kind of you I'm sure," Nell said sarcastically. Even Mary had to laugh.

Just then, the hatch that led to the kitchen opened and a man in a chef's hat poked his head out. "The meeting started?" he asked, and, after some clattering of pots and pans, four canteen workers came out from behind the counter and stood at the back of the room.

Nell declared the meeting open.

"There's only one item on the agenda," she began. "That is the management's plan to bring in more new technology, do away with paper altogether, and make us redundant."

"Just a minute," Terry interrupted, "Excuse me, madam chairman. I don't want to tell you ladies how to run your meeting, but I've got a point of order."

"What is it?" Nell said irritated by this second challenge to her authority.

"As we all know, it is against union rules for non-members to attend meetings . . ."

"Yes, we all know that," Nell said impatiently, "but what's your point of order? That's not a point of order!"

"What about them at the back?" Terry said, pointing rudely at the black workers, who stood their ground.

Nell rose to her feet. Mary was *in extremis*. Something nasty was going to happen. She remembered the way Nell talked about the people who moved into her old house. Terry, she blanked out altogether.

"I have to apologize to the meeting," Nell said calmly. She fiddled inside her handbag again, re-adjusted her spectacles and brought out some papers.

"I am very sorry for not introducing our new recruits. However, what with all the excitement of having two big-wigs here from head office" — the women laughed — "I neglected my duties."

She consulted the papers: "Herbert, Rita, Cynthia and Rose, please come and sit down. There's empty seats up the front. Oh, and just one other thing, before we get on with our business. I don't like being called madam chairman! We're not used to that kind of double talk. I'm not one of them who don't know if she's Arthur or Martha, thank you very much!"

chapter 5

The morning conference, a ritual post-mortem on yesterday's paper, was reduced to a vehicle for Shadbolt's remorseless ego trip. Madeline pictured him secretly watching old Lou Grant videos and practising in front of the mirror. He wore elasticated metal armbands over his shirt sleeves and puffed foul-smelling cigarillos. However, the crucial difference was that while Lou was caring, avuncular and wise, Shadbolt was petty, vindictive, dim-witted, and frequently rat-arsed.

New recruits starting at the paper as junior reporters or sub-editors always took forever to suss just how stupid he was. They couldn't work out how such a berk had risen to the powerful position of editor of a national newspaper.

"Shit always rises," Madeline told them laconically. It would take far too long to explain office politics.

She worked on the news desk as a senior copy taster, picking out the main stories of the night, scrolling them up on a VDU screen, adding instructions for the sub-editors like "cut to half", bring salient facts "higher up" in the story, "get quotes from wife", and so on.

At ten o'clock she and two colleagues, Gordon Jones and one of the trainee graduate kids, would sit down with the night duty editor and get the OK on the lead story and front page. Shadbolt was nowhere to be seen.

The night team worked well together. Madeline and Gordon had it down to state of the art, unerringly selecting the same stories that would be on the front page of every other national daily by monitoring TV and radio news, getting tips from well-paid insiders on other papers and following up on-going stories from the previous day. That was how Shadbolt liked it. He measured success by how closely his front page conformed to those of the rival tabloids. Nothing infuriated him more than seeing his paper with different banner headlines from all the others.

Madeline preferred the night shift. She could go home, forget the paper and forego the dreaded morning conference. The worst possible scenario was working a double shift. Then she had to endure Shadbolt's vile, petulant temper if anything went wrong.

The Japanese proprietor sometimes visited the building, promenading through the machine room and editorial floor with Shadbolt trotting in attendance. Once in a while he stopped to congratulate a reporter or photographer for coverage of a local war, domestic disaster or a juicy scandal. He had it in for the royal family for some reason Madeline couldn't fathom, and loved it when they had marital strife, made gaffes or one of them or their retinue turned out to be gay. The recipients of the owner's praises swelled with pride like small boys who'd been patted on the head and given a sweetie.

Madeline willed the proprietor not to linger at her desk. It had worked so far. She could not be sure how she might react and she badly needed the job.

Distinguished guests came for lunch in the directors' dining room in the reputedly luxurious executive suite upstairs. It disgusted Madeline to see Shadbolt fawning over cabinet ministers, MPs, MEPs, peers, industrialists and city tycoons. Not only because of his obsequious behaviour, but because it offended her that these pillars of society hung out with a man so shallow and smarmy.

Some of the guests at the directors' lunches never figured in the news themselves and their faces would not be familiar to the woman on the Clapham omnibus. Madeline herself had only been able to guess their significance by the regularity and frequency of their appearance at the lunches. Whenever she was around during the day, she made a point of keeping her eyes open and comparing faces with photographs of top civil servants, generals and Privy Counsellors buried in the paper's library files.

On the day of a VIP visit, the directors' lift was cordoned off and a Barbie look-alike in black mini-dress and frilly apron trundled through with drinks trolleys loaded with ice buckets and classy wine bottles. Madeline sensed suppressed excitement coming from the direction of Shadbolt and his cohorts, whose attempt at nonchalance failed dismally. And, sure enough, at precisely one o'clock, two or three shiny, black limos would roll up outside the front door.

A few weeks after her evening at Kitty's, Madeline was doing a double shift, yawning openly as Gordon, a dedicated twitcher, told her all about his bird-watching weekend on the Scillies. As he talked, Gordon automatically marked up stories and scrolled down through the files. The telly was on with the sound turned down when the evening news came on, featuring the Prime Minister wagging a forefinger at a meeting of the captains of industry. Madeline and Gordon had read the speech earlier in the evening when it was released by No. 10 with a 9 pm embargo. There was nothing new in it.

"Dump it?" Gordon said. And without hesitation, Madeline pressed the key which sent the story into the computerized spike basket, recalling the not-so-distant past when there was a big sharp spike poking out of the middle of the old news desk upon which unwanted stories were impaled.

Not long after midnight, Gordon got up and went round the office turning lights off. Madeline adjusted the back of her chair and put her feet up on the desk. The buzz of the old-style newsroom had disappeared forever.

On another floor the paper was made up into pages and if Shadbolt was in the building, he performed the formality of giving it his OK.

Somewhere in a distant office, an old-fashioned typewriter clattered.

"It's that bloody woman again," Gordon grumbled. A clerk in the picture library who was writing a novel about cross-dressing in the 17th century kept them awake every night.

In the gloom, the sound of snores soon drifted over their desks. Through the venetian blinds, she saw the outline of St Paul's broken by the glittering façades of City banks.

Here she was, the wrong side of forty. Long ago she made the decision to learn the business but had been determined not to get stuck in a rut, the royal-watching and boring court cases. The sight of blood made her faint, so gory accidents or crimes were to be avoided, yet she didn't want to cover fashion or style. Her ideal was to achieve the kind of status where she could choose her own assignments: in-depth interviews with women she idolized, great divas, tennis stars and writers. So far life had not gone according to plan. Her job on the paper was ho-hum and her relationship with Carol was drifting into boring hetero-like coupledom.

Carol was a freelance graphic designer who only worked when she felt like it. Mostly she lived on money inherited from her parents who had died a couple of years ago, one after the other in rapid succession, having smoked themselves to death. Madeline was worried about what was going to happen when Carol's money ran out. Nowadays she was drinking more and working less.

In the first flush of new love, they had rushed into getting a mortgage together and now it was getting tougher and tougher to prise Carol's share of the monthly payments out of her.

As Madeline dozed and cogitated on the unfairness of life, the first editions began circulating around the office. Gordon squeezed her shoulder roughly and she jolted fully awake. The fluorescent striplights were blazing and the morning papers were fanned out across the desk. All except theirs carried quarter-page pictures of the Prime Minister's contorted face under two-inch headlines: "Autumn Election: PM Names the Day."

"You're for the high jump," Gordon stuttered.

Madeline's eyes were riveted on their own front page which looked nothing like the mock-up she had seen last night before it went to press.

It was split diagonally. On one side was a picture of the PM with a story mentioning the "possibility" of an autumn election. On the other half, headed by a monster EXCLUSIVE banner, was a story Maddy had never seen in her life before. "Lesbian in Leak Sensation" by Colin Shadbolt.

Madeline stared perplexedly, her thoughts flying backwards and forwards like a pendulum. Obviously, Shadbolt had prepared a front page of his own and substituted it at the last minute. But where the fuck had the lesbian mole story come from? Should she stay and try to ride out the storm, or walk out now and cut her losses? The bottom line was she couldn't afford to lose her job right now. First she had to sort out things with Carol. Jobless, everything would be so much more difficult.

Gordon was wringing his hands and looking pathetic.

"Fuck you, Gordon," she said, "if I go, you go."

"Why hasn't the shit hit the fan already?" he said, shifting from foot to foot. They both looked towards Shadbolt's office. The light was off and there was no sign of life. Okay, Madeline decided to calm down. "That's a good question, Gordon," she said. She would sit tight and wait.

Carol was stretched out on the sofa like the Lady of the Camellias, watching the massive multi-channel satellite TV they hired at great expense. A torn cellophane pack of tortilla chips was spilled out over the rosewood coffee table that had belonged to her mother. Between her thighs she nursed a half-empty bottle of Metaxa left over from their holiday in Greece. One of her late mother's Waterford crystal glasses was balanced delicately on her knee. She didn't look up when Madeline came through the door.

"Not working tomorrow?" Madeline asked, making an effort to sound non-judgemental.

"Nah, it's too hot. Did you see Big Ben stopped again?" Carol said.

"Yeah, it's the heat." Madeline couldn't help herself spewing out useless bits of information she picked up at work.

"It's only the third time since 1911," she said, stopping short of listing the other times, the dates, the reasons for the clock stopping. It interested her that in 1911 it was so hot, ice was delivered to expensive hotels with an armed guard. Once, she'd rescued some dusty glass plate negatives from a place she was working when a basement store was being cleared out. One showed soldiers with guns sprawling on top of a huge ice block on a horse-drawn dray going down Piccadilly.

Carol's eyes did not leave the television screen. She was watching a bright-voiced blonde, wearing thick luminous eye-shadow and a fluorescent pink silk blouse, a type employed by all-night stations to titillate insomniacs into wakefulness between watching repeats of *The Avengers* and forties B-movies.

"Now for a look at this morning's papers," the woman said, winking sassily. Madeline moved aside Carol's pile of Naiad romances and little bags of nuts, put her girlfriend's feet across her knees and settled down to watch.

By this time, all the other papers had picked up Shadbolt's exclusive about the lesbian mole at the Home Office. Now they had footage of her house and the full-scale press siege going on outside it. The more Madeline thought about it, the more obvious it became that there never was a leak. What was being called a leak was in fact a plant. That was why Shadbolt had been so devious. He had already prepared a front page regardless of whatever Madeline and Gordon were doing. Whatever they had come up with would have been substituted. It was a plant, fixed up between Shadbolt and his slimeball political cronies. That was why he was so quick to fire her for spiking the PM's speech, no post mortem, no nothing. It was true Shadbolt hated her guts but sacking her for the election date slip-up was not as clear-cut as it seemed at first. From what she gleaned from the telly, the other papers had based their stories on behind-the-scenes speculation, not on the actual speech itself.

"Guess what?" Maddy said, "I'm going freelance too."

Carol's mouth fell open and the gorgeous thick-lashed eyes which once made Madeline's heart turn over and now had the same effect on her stomach, opened wide. It was the most animated Madeline had seen her for days.

She finally spoke: "What are you talking about?"

"Shadbolt sacked me this morning," Maddy said. She couldn't help feeling pleased to have stirred Carol out of her lethargy. But Carol did not look happy. She took an almighty swig of Metaxa.

"What does it mean? Will you be able to get another job?"

"I don't know, I haven't had time to get my head around it."

"You don't seem too upset," Carol said dismissively.

"I've had a couple of hours to get over it," Maddy told her in a hard voice, "but it wasn't very pleasant being screamed at down the office and called a stupid cunt for everyone to hear!"

Carol's face puckered. "How gross!" she said and put her arm round Maddy's neck, still clutching her drink with one hand and sipping at it every few seconds. Her breath stank of brandy.

"It's OK, honey," said Maddy, "We'll survive. We've still got each other." As the words came out of her mouth Madeline could feel their phoniness hanging in the air like a neon sign and she felt compelled to pat Carol's knee awkwardly.

"I always hated you going into that place," Carol sobbed, "how could I tell my friends where you worked?" Tears poured down her face.

Madeline was shocked. She hadn't realized Carol was ashamed of her work.

Then Carol perked up. "Maybe it's for the best," she said, "now we can get the B&B we've always dreamed about. It must be fate!"

Madeline was sceptical and saw Carol's chin begin to quiver when she replied more sharply than intended: "Fate, my ass. It's because Shadbolt knew I'd be onto that lesbian mole story like a flash. That's why he had to use his tactics of instant dismissal. 'Clear-your-desk-and-get-out-now.' He's been waiting for a reason to say that to me for years."

Carol's chin was quivering again. It was true they had fantasized about a women's B&B, perhaps in Brighton, or even, in their wilder fancies, Greece. But Maddy thought they both knew that's what it was — a pleasant fantasy.

The practical problems were beyond them, even if they managed to raise some cash by selling the house. For one thing, Carol was incapable of going in the kitchen without doing serious damage. Since they had been living together, their entire collection of cheap drinking glasses had been replaced four times, the wooden handles of all their Le Creuset pots had been reduced to charcoal and three kettles burned out.

"You never had any intention of going through with it," Carol accused her, "You've just been humouring me. You know we've always planned it and we were supposed to be working towards it!"

"Let's not argue, I'm tired." Maddy's head hurt.

They both stared at the TV. Carol showed no interest in the plight of the lesbian mole. She cracked pistachios, nibbling angrily, while Madeline waited for her to simmer down so she could raise a different subject.

After several nauseating commercials flickered by, volume blaring, the atmosphere showed no sign of improvement.

Maddy decided to speak before another half-hour segment of *The Twilight Zone* began.

"Can you turn it down a minute?"

With a martyred expression, Carol picked up the remote control switch and fiddled with it irritably till the sound subsided a fraction.

"Remember that night at Kitty's?" Madeline went on.

Carol's back stiffened and she drew up her knees, withdrawing her feet from Madeline's lap. "Of course," she said, "You were chatting up that infant with the spiky hair."

"That's right," Madeline persevered.

"Do you remember the woman you were chatting up? A nice-looking blonde in a grey outfit that might have been a uniform?"

"I was only doing it 'cos Esme said we had to," Carol said defensively.

"Me too," Maddy smiled. "Try to remember. This may be important." She hesitated. "Did you get her phone number?"

Carol reacted badly, as Maddy expected.

"Jesus Christ, Madeline, what do you think I am? Do you think I go round chatting up women and getting their phone numbers while my current lover is sitting not ten feet away?"

Interesting, that use of the word "current", Maddy thought. It made her feel as if she was about to drop off the end of a conveyor belt.

"To be frank," Carol continued, "I've been thinking for some time that you need therapy. Your jealousy and bossiness is getting really oppressive. You've got to work through your stuff, Madeline, there's nothing else for it . . ."

"OK," Maddy said slowly, "I need therapy. Just tell me, did you get the bloody woman's telephone number or didn't you?"

Madeline awoke refreshed. Carol was sleeping as if in a coma, snoring softly with her cupid's bow mouth open. Her photo-sensitive eyes were protected with a black, velvet sleeping mask.

Things weren't so bad, Madeline reflected, she'd been thinking of asking for an unpaid sabbatical so she could make an effort to find work on another paper or maybe in radio or television. In a way, being sacked by Shadbolt was not a bad thing at all. It was more of an accolade. If he liked her, she'd have to ask herself where she was going wrong.

This way, dismissal could be turned to advantage. All she had to do was flesh out the story that was taking shape inside her head, and the quality papers would lap it up. And her by-line would be on all of them. It could lead to work in television. They would be sure to want to interview her — the woman who uncovered the truth about the "Lesbian Mole". God, she was so excited! Why did she feel weak and floppy? Sacked only a few hours and already she had withdrawal symptoms. Pictures of toast dripping with butter and runny yellow egg floated in front of her eyes. She craved the bitter aroma of coffee.

With Carol out for the count, she had the house to herself. She crawled out of bed and made for the kitchen. The refrigerator was stacked with bottles of booze and mixers. No coffee, nothing to make breakfast. She poured herself a 7-Up and took it through to the living room. Nearly everything in the house was Carol's. The place was stuffed with Carol's mother's hideous things.

Olive green, sludge brown, plum-coloured. Heavy velour curtains, velveteen sofa. Dust. In the evenings the old-fashioned standard lamp cast a buttery light which was quite cosy. It would fetch a good price at Camden Lock, but who'd want the heavy three-piece suite?

It would be good to have her own place which she could decorate to her minimalist taste. White walls and woodwork, cream carpet. Black fittings, futon chairs with big primary-coloured cushions and woollen rugs. Plants in terracotta pots. Plenty of light.

chapter 6

Nell was basking in it, acting the Queen Bee. After the meetings she always called out "Who's coming for a jar?" and they all trooped over the road to The Stab in the Back. Somehow she always contrived to close the meetings at 11 am to coincide with opening time.

"Isn't she a great lady?" they said of Nell. "No side to her. What you see is what you get."

Reen didn't join in Nell's praises, so Mary didn't. It had taken Mary a good few months to feel included and become one of the regulars who looked forward to the sociability of the hour or two in the pub.

On the day Terry came, she was relieved to see the two men snapping their brief cases shut and taking their leave shiftily, as if they had other fish to fry. Reen made a crack when she saw them retreating, with their heads down looking at their shoes. "I'll lay you odds, all they got in them bags is the sarnies their wives made them and a copy of *The Sun*," she guffawed.

Mary's admiration for Reen increased, as did her embarrassment that everyone would soon know she was married to the berk from the union.

The Stab was one of the last remaining haunts of the old Fleet Street; all the rest had been turned into wine bars or Karaoke strip clubs. Mary was depressed to see that even The Stab had made an effort at refurbishment. It smelled unfamiliar. The threadbare, urinated-on carpet had been replaced with one that was thick and slippery. The ceiling had been lowered. The bar-staff were kitted out in straw boaters, maroon waistcoats and bow ties.

As they gathered round the bar, the women continued their discussion of the meeting.

"Well, I think he's a bit of all right. He can leave his shoes under my bed any time . . ." one snickered.

The others looked dubious.

"A shit on a swing-swong, if you ask me," Reen said emphatically. "A right C.U.Next Tuesday!"

Mary, who was standing next to her, felt her face flame up. Nell's lizard eyes kept darting towards her. And Mary's vague dislike suddenly crystallized into hatred.

"What'll it be, love?" Reen asked, waving her money over the bar. "Two pints of Guinness," she called without waiting for Mary's reply.

"Jesus, they've only got bottled . . . call this a pub?" The women were all complaining and teasing the young barman. "The pub with no beer . . ."

Whisky Macs, G&Ts lined the counter, "Cheer up love," someone said, "it may never happen."

Reen took charge, carrying both their drinks to a table as far as possible from Nell and her cronies, "I don't trust that cow," she growled.

It only took a few sips of the fizzy bottled Guinness to bring on Mary's exhaustion worse than ever. It was like a concrete block inside her head which she tussled with but couldn't dislodge.

The voices around her were muffled. Their hoots of laughter which usually lifted her spirits made her feel worse.

"Rubes!" Reen called across, trying to make Mary laugh, "I saw a map of Australia down the guvnor's bog this morning. Do you think it means I'm going to have a trip down under?"

Ruby had a knack for reading tea-leaves which she sometimes practised on lavatory bowls.

"Better start packing," Ruby chortled. Mary tried to force a smile.

"What's up with you?" Reen demanded impatiently. "You've been going round like a spare prick at a wedding all morning! Are you with us or ain't you?"

Before Mary could answer, Ruby leaned across and said: "Mary, your bloke's a union man in 'ne? Couldn't you get him to have a go at that poultice what came down this morning?"

Others chimed in, "Yere, worra tosspot."

"Douche bag!"

"That *was* my husband" Mary blurted out then burst into tears.

Ruby's large face crumpled, "Oh sorry love! Me and my big mouth."

But Reen frowned sternly at Mary. "Bloody hell, girl," she said, "It's not the end of the world!"

He was awake. Although he was breathing rhythmically, pretending to be asleep, she could sense him plotting, locked in his world of meetings, manoeuvring, bluffing. A big fish in a small pond. And it was a lost cause.

What would he do when the bosses called his bluff, as she knew they soon would? What would become of her? Both of them would be out of work with no savings and two kids making growing demands.

Terry had no interest in anything other than his union work. It was possible she'd be doing him a favour if she buggered off and dumped the kids on him. That would bring him down to reality with a bang. But every time she thought about the future and the dramatic changes it might bring, her heart began to palpitate and she felt as if she was frightening herself to death.

She tapped him on the shoulder. He could have been a stranger at a bus stop whom she was about to ask the time.

"I know you're awake," she said but he kept quiet. She put her mouth beside his ear.

"Terry . . . do you love the kids?" she whispered.

The bed-clothes jerked as he sat up on his elbow and his voice was furious. "Do I love the kids? What do you mean, do I love the kids? What sort of fuckin' stupid question is that? Why else do I flog my guts out, trying to give them all the things I never had? You're weird, you are. What a fuckin' question."

He rolled himself tightly in the blankets as if to protect himself from her and turned away.

"Well, you never talk to them. You never pick them up," Mary said weakly. The bed-clothes twitched but he didn't answer.

Next morning after he had gone she sat on the bed with her head in her hands not crying but wishing she could. The girl came running in and began whimpering when she saw her mother in distress.

"Mum, mum what is it?" Her desperate, insistent fingers tried to prise Mary's hands from covering her face.

"I'm lonely," Mary said in a muffled voice.

"But you've got me! You've got me!" the girl shouted, jumping up and down. When there was no response to this the child let out an anguished howl and began raining blows on Mary's head with her small fists.

It had been a shit of a week. The kids had gone down with feverish colds and she had to keep them home from school, which meant hardly any rest. Terry started wearing a suit and tie every day which meant extra work ironing shirts. He had been to the barber for a short back and sides and made a great display of shining his shoes every morning. He could never be parted from the briefcase Reen had scoffed at and carried it everywhere with him, like a baby. Everything was getting on her nerves.

To cap it all, Tuesday morning the boy was messing about in the bathroom when there was an ear-splitting scream. He was staring into the handbasin, transfixed. The cold tap was running and trapped in the plughole was a thing like a baby octopus, writhing and twisting. She turned both taps full on and poured bleach over the rubbery thing. It rolled itself into a ball and squeezed down into the plughole, one leg waving in the air. Mary picked up the lavatory brush and, averting her eyes, poked into the basin. When she looked again, it had gone.

After that they were afraid to go to the bathroom all day and relieved themselves in a plastic bowl. The boy said he had been about to brush his teeth and was bending over the basin when he saw the thing come out of the tap.

"It's all over now. It's all gone," Mary soothed him. But she felt as if she were losing her mind. When Terry came home from work he said: "You must have been bloody imagining things. Bloody mad Irish woman!"

"It's not just me," Mary said wearily, "everyone at work's got weird stuff coming out of their taps and little, soft moths in the bathroom."

It was true. First she thought there was something wrong with her eyes. Flying things too soft and fluttery to focus on. When one of them settled on the wall for a second and you pressed it with your forefinger, it dissolved leaving a sooty smudge.

Midnight. She tip-toed down the stairwell to get the night bus in to work. Nell was waiting by the stop.

"Sultry innit?"

"Airless. I feel as though I can't breathe. Jack not giving you a lift in tonight?"

"Wouldn't be standing here would I?" Nell said. She seemed depressed. "Jack's gone all executive-like," she went on. "Got a new suit, works nine to five. I gather him and Tel have done all right for themselves with the new management?"

Mary didn't know what to answer. She wasn't even sure if it was a question. Then the bus came along and they climbed on board. It was humiliating to have to admit she didn't have a clue what Terry was up to. But was Nell really any the wiser or was she just fishing for information?

"I'll tell you one thing for free," Mary said as the bus trundled around St George's Circus. "I'm bloody sick of all the extra ironing."

Nell sneered. "You don't know you're born, girl. When Jack was at *The Times* his overalls got covered with oil and muck every night. Ink used to get in his hair and skin, all over the pillow cases and sheets every night! Used to drip on their heads from off the machines! How would you like to wash that lot?"

Mary ground her teeth. It wasn't her friggin' fault if she wasn't around in those days. She wondered if all their stories were true. They said that in the Wapping plant workers had to wear overalls the same colour as the walls of the area where they worked so they were easy to spot if they strayed anywhere they weren't supposed to be.

According to Reen, Jack was one of the union men who'd wanted to go to Wapping. But the Union got manoeuvred into a strike they couldn't win and Jack had to join it. Nell used to turn up at the pickets in dark glasses to cover up the black eyes Jack had given her. Wouldn't Nell go through the feckin' floor if she found out Mary knew that!

They got down at Ludgate Circus and as soon as they approached the work building, Nell cried: "Jesus, it's a bloody lock-out!"

People were milling and jostling about on the steps. Mary saw

Reen detach herself from the crowd and hurry towards them.

"You'd better make yourself scarce, Your Ladyship," she told Nell, "you've got some hopping mad new recruits waiting to sort you out!"

In all the shouting and confusion, Mary experienced the same panic she'd felt as a child in the playground. She remembered pressing her back against the brick school building, wishing like hell she could disappear between the cracks. The screaming and jumping children were an enigma to her and worse even, a threat. At any moment one of them might drag her into that frightening, unthinking, incomprehensible mass of humanity.

Reen took her arm and she saw Nell hesitate before turning back and disappearing into the dark. She felt like running after her. All she could think of was what Nell hinted about Terry and Jack. "Reen, what's going on?" she whispered.

"We're all sacked, that's what," Reen said. "That bitch must of known. She must of went behind our backs."

Mary resisted when Reen tried to drag her by the arm. "Come on girl," she said, "no-one blames you for what your old man done."

Mary recognized other women cleaners as well as the canteen workers who had joined the union. There were a few journalists too. One of them, that seedy-looking geezer, Gordon something, was wearing a pathetic sandwich board made out of card and string with the word "sacked" filled in with biro.

"This will be a laugh," Reen said as they watched a large man in a Commissionaire's garb approach Gordon.

"You're on private property," said the uniformed man officiously. "I'm afraid I'll have to ask you to move."

"This is a public footway," Gordon stammered. The egg roll he was clutching began to squirt yellow yoke between his twitching fingers.

"You are standing on the company's front door mat," the

Commissionaire said looking down at Gordon. Suddenly Gordon let out a howl of rage, hurled his food on the mat and began dancing up and down on it in a frenzy.

"That's what I think of your fuckin' private property! Thirty-five friggin' years I've flogged my guts out in this bloody place. I've paid your fuckin' wages, you self-important little shit!"

"Go on mate! Tell 'im!" yelled the crowd, gathering round to watch.

"Officer, arrest this man," the Commissionaire called to a young policeman who was yawning nearby, but Gordon suddenly became subdued and pathetic again and everyone went back to standing with their own groups of workmates.

Cynthia, one of the canteen workers, came to speak to Reen. "This is what we get for joining your union," she said bitterly. "That woman Nell recruit us to make up the numbers for sacking."

"You probably would of got the sack anyway," Reen answered. "But we've got to stick together now. Even if we can't get our jobs back, we've got to make a stink. Make the union do something."

All the cleaners gathered round and Mary sensed they looked to Reen.

"Listen," Reen said, raising her voice as if they were having a meeting. "Nell's done a runner and we've got to decide what to do. We don't know for sure what's going on. My guess is when the postie arrives this morning he'll be bringing a goodbye letter from the management. I suggest we meet in the upstairs room at the pub tonight and get ourselves sorted out. In the meantime, I'll get in touch with the union head office and see what I can find out, OK?"

Reen had taken charge. A meeting was arranged for 5 pm. "Do you mean today, like *today* or today like *tomorrow*?" Ruby asked.

"In sixteen hours time, all right? And I want a couple of volunteers to come back to my place now so we can make a start on planning what to do."

Herbert was wearing his chef's trousers and carried his hat folded in a plastic bag. "If you can hang on a few minutes, Reen, we can get something for our breakfast, know what I mean?" he said, winking. He went round to the side entrance and returned a few minutes later, passing right under the eyes of the policeman, with a large paper sack. The cleaners and canteen workers surrounded him, laughing when they saw his load: the nightly delivery of bacon, eggs and bread, intended for the canteen breakfast. "Let's go," said Reen, and Mary tagged along as they piled into Herbert's old van.

chapter 7

The greasy spoon near the vegetable market provided Maddy with a temporary base from which to operate. It was far preferable to expending valuable time and effort shipping out Carol's empties and trying to create a space for herself in the house. The market was bustling and friendly and the elderly Italian couple who ran the caff didn't mind her sitting there all day if she bought a coffee now and then which she did with pleasure, rotating espresso, plain black and cappuccino, no sugar.

There was a pay phone and a pile of dog-eared, eight-year-old phone books in a booth at the back of the shop. When things went quiet between breakfast and lunch, she made her calls.

First she fed £2 coins into the slot and dialled the national Inland Revenue centre in Liverpool, told them she was a freelance reporter, self-employed and elicited from them the code number for the tax office covering Fleet Street. Then she rang the paper, got through to accounts and, adopting a stilted, bureaucratic tone, claimed she was calling from the local tax office. She quoted the correct code, said the computer in Liverpool had gone down and they'd lost some of their records. In particular, one of the part-time cleaners employed by the paper. They knew they should have twelve names and they only had eleven.

Maddy cleared her throat, "Please read out the twelve names so I can check them off my list and see which one is missing."

After a few minutes, while Maddy hunched over the phone biting her lip, the clerk returned.

"We had fifteen cleaners, not twelve," she said in a disgruntled voice.

"Oh dear, it's worse than we thought," Maddy ad-libbed. She wanted to ask why the woman had used the past tense. But perhaps it wasn't significant. The voice on the other end summoned up a pouting teenage face seen through the grille in the cash and pay office during regular arguments over expenses the paper owed her. Always a bloody battle to get peanuts out of the bastards. And the airhead pouter always acted like it was her own money she was giving away.

"Just read the names through quickly, please my love, will you?" Maddy said, and tapped her pencil impatiently. She was getting into the role.

There were two Marys and Madeline wrote down their names and addresses and NHS numbers in a small hard-covered notebook obtained especially for the purpose. It was very satisfying.

The spotty mirror in the phone booth was not ideal for a style check but she always looked good with a tan and the long, hot summer had burnished her skin and lightened her hair. Bra-less under a turquoise tank top, she wore well-cut cotton twill pants with turnups and her sharpest cream jacket hung over the back of her chair. The right mix of smart and casual, she thought, as she picked up the phone again and dialled the number of a distant acquaintance, a friend of a friend, who worked on an upmarket women's magazine. Even though she knew it had recently been acquired by the same man who owned the paper she'd just been sacked from, she wasn't deterred. They were different worlds. It was like owning a sausage factory and an ice-cream factory, she reasoned. The workers in the ice-cream factory did not know anything about the workers in the sausage factory and vice versa. And, if there were any problems, she could write under another name. Gloria Spicer was one she'd used before and liked. So an appointment was fixed for Gloria with the woman at the magazine for four o'clock. Another satisfactory piece of business accomplished.

On impulse, she dialled again. This time, her own number. Carol's brisk business voice recorded on the Ansaphone months ago made her wince. It was shocking to realize how badly her lover had deteriorated in such a short time.

"This is the number for Carol Brown and Madeline Silver. There is no-one to come to the phone at the moment . . ." Maddy imagined Carol lying senseless under the duvet . . . "but if you'll leave your name and number after the tone, we'll get back to you," the old Carol's voice finished brightly.

Near tears, Madeline spoke painfully, "Listen sweetheart, it's me. I hate telling you this way, but I'm moving out. Our relationship's just no good any more."

She dropped the phone and went back to her cluttered table. Now she was deflated, her decisiveness utterly depleted.

The small caff began filling up and a queue formed at the counter for takeaways. When she looked at her watch she was horrified to see it was almost twelve-thirty. If she didn't move her ass, Carol might get up and play the Ansaphone before she had time to get home and erase the message.

"Always hang on to your legs love," said the woman at the bus stop, "otherwise you'll end up like me. Can't get about. Take my advice, hang on to your legs."

"I'll try to," Maddy smiled pleasantly, hoping the bus would come soon. A man was pissing in the doorway of a nearby boarded-up laundrette. It was funny. Since she'd stopped working she'd been observing in the flesh, so to speak, some of the stories she'd worked on sitting in the office: stories she had never experienced and only half believed. She remembered subbing one about the closure of public loos and how it had led to even more men pissing in public.

Madeline felt a firm grip on her arm. "You can't beat our boys marching, they're the best in the world!"

"Is that right?"

A stream of pee snaked towards them. "Excuse me," Madeline said, "I think this is a request stop." She disengaged herself and stepped into the road to flag down the bus. She helped the woman get her zimmer frame on board, then made for the upstairs deck not wishing to be trapped into further conversation.

"No-one's going to treat me like cunt. Not any more. No fucker's going to use me for cunt. They can fuck off!"

Madeline winced. She had sat down in front of two more nutters. London was full of them. It was impossible to move about the city without being assailed from all sides. How come she had failed to notice how much things had changed? She blamed it on working strange, unsocial hours in the twilight zone of the office. But she couldn't resist the conversation going on behind her and strained her ears.

"It's none of your fuckin' business what I do. I'll make up my own mind what I'm going to do. No fucker's going to tell me what to do. That's the difference between you and me. Nobody uses me for cunt. No fucker, so you can just shut your mouth."

After a few moment's silence the quieter voice said:

"I'm not trying to tell you what to do, Vlasta. I'm just asking you to be careful, that's all."

There was no need to strain her ears to catch the explosive reply.

"Careful! Me! Look who's talking! What about that fuckin' Rainey!"

Now Maddy's ears were aching with the effort of concentrated eavesdropping. Rainey! Could it be one and the same?

"You can leave her out of it," the quieter voice went on. "It's not like you with your fuckin' boyfriends."

"Boyfriends! I only took them in 'cos they're gay and I wanted to help. You try to help someone out and they shit on you. I'm not having it no more. Know what I mean? No fucker . . . I can live on my own. I don't need the money. I can fuckin' live on me own. You can leave tonight."

Snuffling sounds.

"I want me fuckin' money back then!"

"Nobody uses me, no fucker . . ."

"Shshsh . . . I'm only tryin' to tell you for your own good. That Joe's a fuckin' psychopath. He's goin' to do you in one day."

"Well, when it happens, then I'll fuckin' know won't I? Everyone has to find out for themselves, so keep your fuckin' trap shut. I can fuckin' look after myself. I don't need you!"

"Don't let that fuckin' mad bastard hurt you Vlasta. That's all I'm tellin' you. The fuckin' maniac will do you in."

"Who's fuckin' talkin'? Who's fuckin' callin' who mad? What about yourself? You're so fuckin' thick I have to tell you everything four times before you can take it in . . ."

After more sniffs and snuffles, Maddy feared the conversation had petered out. Then the same voice continued.

"What about that fuckin' Rainey? I told you eighteen months ago. How long did it take you to catch on? Don't you talk about fuckin' mental. You should be in fuckin' mental hospital yourself? What's wrong with it? I've been in and out all my life."

"What! Mental?"

"Of course fuckin' mental. You know that. You visited me twice."

"But I didn't know you'd been in and out all your life.'

"What about it? Everyone should go. Your trouble is you're

too fuckin' thick to get in. They wouldn't have you. You're too thick."

After a few minutes silence, the softer voice spoke.

"Isn't this your stop?"

"No. I'm going to the top today. Your skin's very dry this morning. You should put something on it."

More snuffling: "I shouldn't use soap on my face. Not with my skin. I put Johnson's baby oil on it last night and it was all right but when I washed it this morning it's gone dry again. I shouldn't use soap on me face."

Both had dropped their voices so she had to close her eyes to make out what they were saying.

"Come round the caff and I'll give you your rent," whispered the snuffler.

"How can I get all the way down there and back in me fuckin' break?"

"Get a taxi."

"OK."

"And I'll see you tonight. But don't go telling me what to fuckin' do. Right? Know what I mean? Like with you and Rainey. How long did it take you? Eighteen fuckin' months. And you wouldn't listen to me would you."

"I didn't know what she was like. Then she disappeared. Told me she was visiting her mum."

"Visiting her mum! Ha! Ha! She even tried it on with me. That night you brought her to the club she came sidling up to the piano and asked me out to dinner while you were at the bar getting her a drink!"

"You went . . .?"

"Just to dinner, I went. That's the difference between you and me. I know what I'm doing. You don't fuckin' know what you're doing."

"It's nice to have somebody . . ."

"*Have* somebody! I don't need *no* fucker. So don't get any ideas. Just don't try to tell me what to fuckin' do and don't fuckin' interfere in my life."

"You'll find out the hard way."

"That's it!! That's what I'm trying to fuckin' tell you. You found out about Rainey the hard way and that's the only way anyone finds out anything — the fuckin' hard way. So you leave me alone to get on with it."

Madeline turned her face to the window as the bus juddered to a halt near King's Cross and, behind, near the aisle, someone got up and climbed off the bus. A portly shape in a battered oil skin anorak, incongruous in the heat, passed beneath the window and briefly looked up with a diffident smile.

After a few moments Madeline could contain herself no longer and she moved back to sit beside the woman behind her who was staring straight ahead as if in a trance.

"Excuse me," Madeline said tentatively, and the woman swivelled a pair of demonic eyes in her direction. "I couldn't help overhearing some of what you and your friend were saying and I'm desperately trying to track down an old friend of mine called Rainey . . ."

Before she could say more Vlasta shouted:

"You fuckin' middle-class bitch! How dare you listen to other people's private conversations . . ."

Madeline thought she was going to be hit and made for the lower deck with her heart pounding. As feet pumped down the stairs, she heard: "You bitches think your shit don't smell. But it does!"

She jumped off as soon as the doors opened at the next stop and walked as fast as she could without looking back.

How dare that fuckin' low-life bitch call her middle class! She grew up on the Nye Bevan estate, went to fuckin' Skeggy for family holidays, even though it seemed like another world now.

How she despised the working class for their supine spinelessness and stupidity! The bingo, the telly crap, Mills and Boon, tits and bums. How they lapped it all up! Holidays in freezing, breeze-block cabins by the freezing, heaving sea. Grey, grey, grey.

And still they thought they were the greatest in the world. Her father, a lifelong CP member, always said "The British working class is the most advanced in the world" — "So how come they haven't had a revolution?" Madeline had taunted him. She had dedicated her youth to getting out of the squalid little Salford back-to-back where her mother still lived. Not long after her escape, her father had died quietly on a barstool in the local, a pint of bitter on the counter in front of him. "Died with his boots on," her mother repeated, as if, to her, it meant something profound. On one of her rare visits to see her mother Maddy had once asked, "How do you feel about the collapse of the Soviet Bloc, after all, you devoted your whole life to the Communist Party?"

"No use crying over split milk," her mother said.

Soon she was at The Angel. When she turned the corner into their street the air was full of flying things. Her things. Neighbours who were grouped around the doorstep jumped out of the way as a television set hurtled to the pavement. Clothes. CDs. All in the road. A pile of books lay with their spines broken. Her precious SCUM *Manifesto*, the original edition, lay in tatters, pages fluttering into the drains. Her beloved headline collection: a scrapbook of her favourite front pages, flew out of the window. BEEB MAN SITS ON LESBIAN! BEAM ME UP POOFY!

Kids with serious faces rode their bikes in figures of eight outside the house. Carol's wild, putty-coloured face appeared at the top window and let fly with Madeline's yucca plant. Madeline could see the saddle of sallow skin across her nose and upper lip, sure sign of a bout of heavy drinking.

She was haunted by Vlasta's voice. Learn the fuckin' hard

way. How true it was! All her friends had told her Carol was the wrong woman for her and she had never listened. She'd gone ahead and found out, like Vlasta said, the fuckin' hard way.

Keeping her head down, Madeline crossed the road and trudged past the flats on the opposite side. She was too depressed even to make the effort to rescue her belongings and she couldn't face a showdown with Carol. She had hours to fill in until four o'clock and nowhere to go.

She was almost crying as she stumbled along the street. "Everybody needs somebody," she mumbled to herself.

chapter 8

Because of the extreme heat Wimbledon had been postponed until September and even then the temperature on centre court was in the nineties. For twenty years, Rosemary had attended the women's final with her friend Helen Ashmole, whom she had known at boarding school. Helen now lived in Portsmouth and was married to a sub-lieutenant in the Royal Navy who spent long spells at sea.

Rosemary had no particular feelings towards Helen though she valued their friendship for its longevity and reliability. Contact was infallibly regular, cards and letters were exchanged at Christmas and birthdays and, when one took the initiative to write, the other would respond by return post.

Rosemary did not expect to hear from Helen after the scandal broke. However, as neither of them had a birthday at that time of year and their annual tennis date did not take place in June for reasons beyond their control, there was no reason for Helen to make contact.

It bucked Rosemary up considerably when in late August a square, violet envelope, addressed in Helen's neat up-and-down hand, fluttered through the letter box like a beautiful butterfly and landed on top of a pile of junk mail. Inside there was the ticket for the women's final and a perfectly correct note, not gushing but warm, trusting she and her mother were well and looking forward to the tennis.

Rosemary experienced a sudden rush of affection for Helen

and felt that her long ordeal was at last coming to an end. The telephone had ceased to shrill constantly, and when it did it was only the occasional request for an "in-depth" interview, whatever that might be.

Life was returning to something resembling normality. There were even compensations. She no longer had to endure Miss Alexander's irritating little ways. Her salary continued to appear on her bank statement every month, pending an internal inquiry which, Rosemary had made up her mind, she would refuse to attend, even if it meant criminal charges were brought against her. However, in the latter case, she was confident of fully refuting them as there was not a shred of evidence that she had committed even the merest indiscretion.

Celeste was back after one of her frequent Friday night jaunts into London from which she usually returned pink-cheeked and hyper.

"Rosie!" called the corncrake voice Rosemary loathed but knew she might miss some day.

"Rosie!"

"Mother, please don't call me that. Daddy named me Rosemary and that's the name I prefer to be known by, if you don't mind," she said firmly.

"Tommyrot! The minute your father found out you were a girl he completely lost interest in the whole business. Dear, lovely man that he was, no-one could accuse him of being domesticated. The only babies he ever kissed were the ones thrust upon him on official occasions. Goodwill, you know."

The trip to London must have taken it out of Celeste. She was lying on a plump lavender bedspread with her silk stockings (she eschewed nylon) rolled down and her tiny legs akimbo. The bedroom walls were soft lilac with pale blue woodwork and a white marbled fireplace. There were delicate Chinese and

Indian vases and ornaments. And next to the bed, a brass table, each corner wrought into the face of the elephant god, Ganesh, with jewels for his eyes, the trunks forming his legs.

"Cut my toenails for me will you, Rosie," Celeste demanded in a child's voice, holding out a pair of clippers. And, without a word, Rosemary peeled off her mother's silk stockings and began tending the feathery blue-veined feet.

Celeste, after all, was helpless. For her age, she was spry and alert, but could do nothing for herself because she had never needed to, and it did not occur to her to start now.

They had a woman in three times a week who cleaned, washed and ironed. Rosemary drove her white hatchback to the massive supermarket in Tunbridge Wells every Saturday morning and ineptly filled cardboard boxes with food.

"Mother, tomorrow I'll go shopping on my own. I want to leave early in the morning to avoid the hordes."

Celeste always slept early and rose late. She made a slight *moue* of disappointment. But Rosemary was now massaging the soles of her feet, tired from trotting the pavements of Wigmore Street and Marylebone Lane where she and her ancient cronies haunted the once-fashionable patisseries.

Rosemary observed her mother's drooping eyelids. The old girl was in no condition for an argument.

"Time for your nightie."

Celeste fought to stay awake as Rosemary eased her into a soft woollen shift and pulled the bedclothes up to her daily-plucked chin.

The weekly supermarket ordeal would be somewhat less tiresome without Celeste piling up the trolley with unsuitable purchases and prying into other people's shopping trolleys.

"Lights out in the dorm," Rosemary murmured as she tiptoed from the room.

Celeste ate like a bird, pecking at tiny snacks of cambozolla on wafers or a portion of taramasalata topped with a teaspoon of supermarket caviare with dainty fingers of toast. Rosemary was a hearty eater but had never learned to cook. Her secret vice was fish and chips which she devoured furtively straight from the paper sitting in her car in a side street. She was irritated by Celeste's habit of fixing herself finickety little treats at frequent intervals during the day. Her mother always insisted on using the finest, most delicate china, which could not be put in the dish washer, instead of the sturdy cups and plates Rosemary had bought for everyday use. And she allowed her cat, the old Russian Blue, Pud, to eat from porcelain bowls.

"If you have to indulge the animal," Rosemary observed one morning at breakfast, "why not designate a dish and make sure she uses the same one for every meal? Then wash it thoroughly in hot soapy water."

"She needs her toothie-pegs cleaned," Celeste said. "Did you know most pussies die simply because they cannot chew their food properly?"

"What rot," Rosemary said, smoothing her newspaper. The crossword was a tough one.

"Dental technology has not kept pace with the longevity of the modern human either," Celeste went on. "My body has outworn my teeth even though my gums are healthy . . ."

"Hmmm . . . so you are a modern human are you?"

"More up-to-date than some more recent models I could mention," replied Celeste. "And by the way, Puddy needs to go vetty wetty . . . will you take her?"

"Oh mother, do I have to?"

A few mornings later Rosemary awoke to find she had slept later than usual. She leapt out of bed and hurriedly showered. Today she had a lunch appointment with Helen and she hated to be late. They had arranged to meet at Chez Solange in

London, their first meeting for months.

When she came out of her bathroom wrapped in a fluffy towel her eye was immediately drawn to the new Italian suit which she had laid out on the bed in readiness to try on and, if suitable, wear to lunch.

She hated the changing rooms of department stores and needed to try clothes in the privacy of her own bedroom in front of the full-length mirrors in which she could see her back when she unfolded the wardrobe doors. Even in Harrods the attendants were over-attentive and didn't respect one's need for privacy. She was horrified to find that the changing rooms nearly everywhere else were communal these days.

The trousers of the new suit had acquired a peculiar sheen. Curiously she picked them up and, as she did so, liquid dribbled onto her bare toes and the unmistakable odour of cat urine stung her nostrils.

Ever since Rosemary had stopped working, Pud had tormented her by making puddles wherever they would cause the maximum distress. However, it seemed impossible that the geriatric animal, whose legs could hardly carry her, could have leapt onto the bed to perform this latest outrage. Rosemary knew Celeste would only laugh and wag her finger. "Naughty girl," she always cooed in a proud, adoring tone, and Pud would screw up her button eyes and settle her flat face into her neck like a contented owl.

But on this occasion, Rosemary decided she had had enough. She ripped a handful of tissues out of a box on the dresser and dabbed the carpet. The purple and gold carrier bag in which she had bought the trousers was still hanging from the doorknob of her walk-in wardrobe and she grabbed it and stuffed the trousers and tissues into it before getting back under the shower to sluice herself down furiously.

The smell of cat urine was pervading and degrading. She

shuddered as she remembered the occasion Sir Gregory sent her to visit one of the department's secretaries who was terminally ill. The woman lived in a basement flat in Belsize Park with five cats. As Rosemary stepped into the dank hall she almost gagged. She pushed a bunch of flowers into the woman's hands and fled. God knows how she was going to get her bedroom back to normal. She slipped into her familiar cream silk dressing gown and went barefoot down the hall to Celeste's room. The old woman was fast asleep and Pud nowhere to be seen.

The small study at the back of the house overlooked a pleasant garden which was well-kept by a local unemployed youth who demanded payment in cash. Telephone books were piled underneath the escritoire and Celeste refused to allow Rosemary to move them as they were a convenient height upon which to rest her feet. So Rosemary had to get down on her hands and knees to find the yellow pages book and, on standing up, cracked her skull on the desk. The smarting, stubbed-toe-like pain was further provocation and justification for what she was about to do. She knew it would hurt Celeste but felt no remorse as she ran her shaking finger down the list of local veterinary surgeons.

A charming young receptionist recommended taking Pud to a privately-run cats' home where she could live out her last days in peace and luxury. "We are not here to put animals down," she said, "we are here to improve the quality of their lives and if your cat is perfectly healthy there doesn't seem to be any reason why she should not be allowed to enjoy the twilight of her life until nature takes its course, wouldn't you say?"

"It's just that my mother is too frail to look after her any longer," Rosemary demurred. "And I don't have the time."

Finally it was agreed that an appointment would be made for Pud to be received at the cats' home: Rosemary felt irritation rise again when she realized this would entail a long drive up to Cambridgeshire.

"Isn't there a nearer place?" she said, trying to smother her annoyance. She could hear Celeste moving about in her bedroom and making clucking noises to the cat.

"I'm afraid not," the receptionist said.

"Very well, ask them to put it to me in writing will you, with all the costs involved."

She put the phone down and dialled again, this time a local carpet cleaning firm. As she waited for someone to pick up the phone she had second thoughts. Was it worth having the cleaner do the work before Pud was disposed of? Where would she sleep while the room was still smelly? She could stay the night in London, book in at a hotel. It would make a welcome break from being confined with Celeste day after day. Yes, she desperately needed to get away from mother for a while. The old girl was surpassing herself in battiness.

Rosemary realized she was not coping well with her enforced early retirement. Her nerves were shot to pieces by the attentions of the gutter press and the subsequent lack of attention was also nerve-wracking in its own way. It was as though the Rosemary they had created, defiant, shocking and sexual, had ceased to be, died perhaps, and the real Rosemary had begun to mourn her a little.

A few hours later she was seated opposite Helen in a quiet back room in the restaurant scrutinizing the menu. Helen sipped sparkling Australian Chardonnay from a long-stemmed flute.

"I saw a young man throw himself in front of a train. He was standing right next to me," Helen said conversationally.

"When?"

"On the way here," she replied with a faint smile. "I came by underground from Waterloo."

"Are you all right?"

"Well, it was an *hour* ago. But it certainly makes one think . . ."

"Think about what?"

"You know, Rosemary. One's mortality, that sort of thing."

"One thinks about it constantly," Rosemary said. "You seem to forget, I am cooped up all day with a pre-corpse."

"Ugh, what a morbid expression," Helen shuddered. "It sounds as though you need a complete break from everything. How long is it since you had a proper holiday?"

Rosemary looked up. "I hate going abroad," she said. "I think the world would be a better place if everyone stayed home in their own backyards and minded their own business."

"I wasn't suggesting a colonizing mission," Helen said. "Just a couple of weeks lying on some beautiful beach far from anyone who knows you or whom you know."

"Everyone's forever telling me what I need and what I don't need," Rosemary snapped.

"Everyone?" Helen queried craftily. "Who's everyone?"

She felt too ashamed and embarrassed to confide in Helen about the circulars which had been coming through the letter box from the Sexual Redemption Trust offering counselling to enable her return to nature's normal heterosexual path. Instead, she replied, "Celeste. Celeste is everyone." Of course, there was no "everyone" in her life.

"My mother's cat is determined to drive me out of the house," she went on, changing the subject. "She uses my bedroom as a urinal and Celeste won't do a thing about it."

"Poor you . . ."

"I thought of booking in to Claridges for a couple of nights while my carpet is being cleaned, using the time to catch up on some concerts and galleries, and we've got Wimbledon next week . . ." The waiter came over and they both ordered fresh asparagus and Rosemary, who was ravenous, asked for bread.

Helen had once played the oboe in an all-woman symphony orchestra. She had lovely green eyes and went to a salon every morning to have her face made up for the day. All she had to do was dab at the finished picture with a piece of cotton wool whenever she felt the heat affecting the surface, which she now did with the aid of a tiny mirror from her hand-bag. With the pointed tip of her tongue she renovated her lipstick.

"Everyone's been dazzled by the publicity surrounding you, Rosemary," Helen said in an admiring tone. "I don't think you realize. All those demonstrations, those amazing scenes outside your house and you've been so modest and retiring throughout everything. You're a celebrity. We've all been utterly *dazzled*. And I won't hear of you booking into a hotel," she murmured, leaning across the table. "We can use Roger's flat in Harley Street."

Rosemary froze, a morsel of food half-way to her lips.

"No, I can't." she said.

Helen laughed. "What on earth do you imagine I'm suggest-ing?" she said with her eyebrows raised.

Rosemary wanted to bolt. And then, to her horror, Helen reached over and placed her hand over hers. Rosemary drew back as if she'd been scalded.

"Don't ever do that again," she stammered, eyes round. "Or we cannot continue to be friends."

Helen sat back and sipped her wine. After a few moments contemplation she spoke. "It's a great pity you never married," she sighed, "a great pity, because you could have saved yourself all this anguish."

"What do you mean?"

"What I mean is, things are not always as they appear. If one wishes to keep up appearances, one can. Roger and I, for example, have a very convenient understanding. Very convenient."

When Rosemary arrived home Celeste was rocking in her chair with Pud curled up on her knee.

"You don't look very happy, Rosie. I thought you were staying over with that lovely girl, Helen?"

"Staying over! Who said so?" She eased off her shoes and flopped into an armchair opposite her mother.

"I do miss a nice fire," Celeste said, wistfully, eyeing the empty hearth. "Do you think the weather will ever return to normal?"

"Listen to me, mother. I'm sleeping in the spare room tonight and first thing in the morning, I'll take Pud to the vet."

"Oh, hear that Puddy," Celeste said delightedly. "She loves you after all. Rosie Posy is going to take Puddy Wuddy to have her toothie pegs cleaned."

"Sometimes I think you care more for that damned animal than you do for me," Rosemary said in a wobbly voice.

"What a silly girl you are," Celeste said, stroking the cat. "You say the silliest things sometimes."

"Mother, you'd better listen to me and take me seriously," Rosemary commanded. "I have reached an important decision concerning my future. It is nothing whatever to alarm oneself over. Things will continue in exactly the same vein as before. However, I have to tell you, I have decided to get married."

Celeste's bejewelled fingers ceased moving in the cat's shaggy fur.

"That won't fool anyone, dear," she said softly.

"Have that damned cat ready in the morning," Rosemary ordered, as she left the room.

chapter 9

A clammy smog hung over the Thames. Through the train window Madeline could barely make out the dockland skyline. Shafts of ochrous sunlight ricocheted off the buildings. It was years since she'd been to the docklands and everything was shabbier. For as long as she could remember, the cranes had been there and a new generation of workers in hard hats toiled beside the railway.

She prepared herself mentally as best she could for an interview, and to put herself in the right frame of mind to sell herself. But she felt more like topping herself. For hours she'd been travelling on buses and trains. She was dirty and tired. What a relief to get out of the airless carriage! Even though the river flowed thick and mucoid, it was comforting to be near water.

The women's magazines recently acquired by the Japanese publisher were now all housed under one roof at Canary Wharf. She entered a rocket-shaped glass elevator. It shot vertiginously up the centre of the building, so she could see all round the open-plan galleries as she passed on her soundless journey. Then it stopped and the doors slid open. She gritted her teeth and dared not look down as she stepped out onto a narrow moving walkway. This swept her across space to the offices she wanted.

Everything was powder pink and grey with gold trimmings. She went to the bathroom to check her personal hygiene and, thank the goddess, there was every facility a woman could wish

for. How she'd love to work in a place like this! She turned on
the brass taps and out came beautiful, chemically treated, clean
hot water. Bliss! There were sachets of shampoo, soap,
deodorant, little disposable combs, toothbrushes, tampons and
tissues.

One of her first-ever jobs had been on a women's magazine in
grotty old offices in Long Acre; it was part of the same group of
publications which had been launching new titles, letting them
go bust and acquiring others for decades: teenage pulp, true
romances, comics, scientific and trade papers. Maddy (who was
still trying to go over to calling herself Madeline) had acquired
the diminutive of her name while she was a teenager at the Long
Acre job. She started out as a general dogsbody, making tea for
the bosses (all women) and running messages. One of her regular
duties was to fetch sandwiches and coffee from an Italian deli in
Drury Lane. As the junior member of staff, a kid with her hair in
bunches and skirt up to her fanny, she was treated as a cute
mascot and acted accordingly, recognizing that it was dangerous
to appear too smart and ambitious for her kinky boots. By day
she was the office ingénue, by night a leather-clad pillion pussy,
in the Gateways till all hours. Weekends she was at the demos:
the Bunny Club, Miss World, the American Embassy.

Her department was responsible for hiring models for fashion
shows to promote the magazine in department stores and at
Agricultural Shows around the country. Music from the forties
and fifties was specially selected to lure in the matrons. They
also co-ordinated special offers which were usually mail-order
clothing: some were ready-made garments and others were bits
of material already cut out, to be sewn up by the reader. There
was intense competition in the rag trade to win contracts for
special offers. Suppliers of textiles, sweatshop owners and
makers of buttons and yarn, all competed for Maddy's boss's
favour. In turn, the boss was always looking over her shoulder.

Afraid a younger rival may step into her shoes, she would never dare take a holiday or stay at home when ill.

The place was unionized from top to bottom, from journalists and secretaries to highly-skilled artists and pattern-cutters. It had been Maddy's dearest wish to obtain an NUJ card.

When a vacancy arose on the team who answered readers' problems under the collective nom-de-plume Jennifer Cavendish, Maddy applied. For the interview, she dispensed with the bunches, swept her hair back and and squeezed into a tube skirt. She was given a test which consisted of writing replies to as many letters as possible in forty-five minutes and passed with flying colours. Not only had she produced the highest number of letters but her extensive knowledge of women's resources meant quality as well as quantity. Thus had Maddy cut her journalistic eye teeth on the misfortunes of women whose husbands beat them, prematurely ejaculated, and screwed around, women whose offspring were ungrateful, whose bodies did not conform to the norm as portrayed in women's magazines and all of whom wondered where they were going wrong.

After refreshing herself in the powder room, Madeline felt restored enough to face the interview. The editor's room was semi-circular, built out over the river, with a spectacular view. And the editor was curled up in a large, white leather armchair. She looked to be in her early twenties.

"Hiya, Gloria, take a seat," she said flapping a hand. Madeline lowered herself onto a matching sofa which oomphed out air as she sat on it. There was no desk in the room and she couldn't see a telephone. She crossed her ankles, trying to relax under the girl's candid stare. She was at a disadvantage, immediately sensing herself in the presence of exactly the kind of woman who made her feel inadequate and ungraceful: middle-class, self-assured, shit wouldn't melt in her mouth, devoid of self-doubt, exactly the type Vlasta had unjustly accused *her* of being. Without even knowing her.

"I can't remember if we've met before. My name's Sarah."

Madeline was tongue-tied. However it didn't matter because Sarah did not leave her an opening to speak.

"As you may have noticed, this is no longer a labour-intensive business, Gloria. Everything is done electronically. We get most of our stories from a central computer and they are updated, subbed if necessary, and type-set by a very small team. We rotate the topics so we don't duplicate ourselves and we use agency features when appropriate. We get our pictures from a central library. So, basically, what I'm telling you, Gloria, is that we don't need freelancers. Have you got a Tandy?"

"No, couldn't I post stuff in?"

Sarah smiled, "Postage is for plebs, Gloria. If you can get hold of a Tandy, I could suggest a few stories we haven't got covered and might consider paying for, if you can come up with the goods."

"I'll get a Tandy," Madeline said.

Sarah pressed a buzzer with her foot. In came a secretary. "Get me the project file, please, Tracey." A printer fluttered for a few seconds and Tracey was back with a flimsy sheet of paper.

"Let's see. Packs of dogs roaming council estates, does that grab you? No? Woolies cut a woman's bonus to pay for a forty-year gold watch and she gets a six-month suspended sentence for fiddling the equivalent from the payroll when she retired. We'd like to follow that up some time. Interested? More women are getting involved in ram-raids and traffic rows, there have been fights in car parks. We could give you some background to go on . . . what else? Remember yuppies? Well a whole bunch of them moved out of London in the eighties and set up an alternative community in Norfolk, everything high tech. You'd have to pay your own fare up there."

"You couldn't give me an advance or a contract?"

"Sorry Gloria, no way. Take it or leave it."

"Can I ring you tomorrow?"

"Better tell me yes or no right now. I'm hard to get hold of."

"OK. I'll take the Woolies and the yuppies."

"Fine. Pick up the background from Trace on your way out."

The interview was over.

As she climbed the stairs to Kitty's for the third time that week, she told herself it was to look at the noticeboard for rooms to let, but in fact it was out of compulsion to see Carol again even though she knew it would be painful. Since the day Carol threw her belongings in the street, Madeline had dossed down with friends. She had not communicated with Carol except through Carol's solicitor. Madeline did not have a solicitor.

It was a quiet night with no entertainment and no sign of Esme. When Madeline was depressed, Billie Holiday did her head in. She asked the woman behind the bar to change the music to something less doleful. Ferron started up, which was even worse. How eighties!

In her straitened circumstances, Madeline could only afford half a lager. Perhaps a well-heeled friend might show up and offer her a short? She wandered over to read the cards pinned to the back wall. "Fourth woman to share large, communal house in Brixton. Vegetarian. N/S. Must like cats and children." Definitely not.

"Large room in women-only house in Stoke Newington . . ." she took down the details. "Share comfortable house with one other woman in Islington. C/H. All mod cons." Madeline looked again at the telephone number. It was Carol's, the bitch! She was supposed to be putting the house on the market, not letting out rooms.

Kitty's was filling up. Madeline grabbed an empty table and

sat listening in misery to Ferron droning on.

Seeing Carol's ad was a setback. All day she'd been trying to pull herself up by the bootstraps. Think positive.

Carol was going to buy her out and she tried ringing the solicitor to get some money in advance. After all, Carol was still living in the house and Madeline had the expense of living elsewhere. Compensation was due for the possessions Carol had smashed. With the money forthcoming, she planned to buy a laptop. But there was no money forthcoming. The solicitor was nasty and told her: "Stop harassing Carol."

Maybe, if she could get the fare together to go to Norfolk to cover the yuppy commune, she could deliver the copy to Sarah by hand. No, that wouldn't work. Now she remembered why it had to be sent by computer: there was no-one to type it into the frigging system! Tomorrow, she would try the bank manager. Without a laptop she couldn't operate.

A woman came over and sat opposite. Madeline stared.

"Never seen a dyke in uniform before?" Rainey said.

"A cat may look at a Queen."

"Flattery will get you everywhere. Can I refresh your glass?"

"Does a bear shit in the woods! I badly need a scotch."

Maybe her luck was changing.

Rainey had a terrific body under the grey twill, Madeline could tell. And a lovely little heart-shaped face and Bambi eyes. When she came back with the drinks, Madeline cleared her throat. "I'm financially embarrassed at the moment, but I'll make all this up to you by and by." Rainey responded with a flirtatious smile. Encouraged, Madeline went on, "You know, I've seen you round. Once here, the night Esme showed us how to chat women up, and a couple of times outside the place where I used to work. You were delivering VIPs."

Rainey looked interested. "Where's that?"

"A newspaper office in Farringdon."

"Ah, yes," Rainey laughed, "the boozy lunches." She had a nicely-modulated voice, pitched low, which appealed to Madeline. Soon she found herself telling Rainey all her business. The split from Carol, the interview with Sarah.

"Even if they do pay for my work, I'd have to sign over exclusive rights. It's an old con. They give you a cheque, you have to sign on the back, and in small print underneath is a waiver giving them full copyright. If you don't sign, their bank won't honour the cheque."

"Does it matter?" Rainey asked. "I mean, is your stuff so sought after round the world?"

"Maybe it will be . . . if I could just sell this one story I've got in mind," Madeline said.

"Sounds interesting," Rainey said politely.

Madeline hesitated, on the brink of telling Rainey all about the lesbian civil servant. Then she remembered Vlasta. If Rainey had such low-life friends, caution was in order.

"I met a friend of yours the other day," she began. Rainey looked curious.

"Have you been following me about?" she said.

Madeline detected slight irritation. Slow down. She was taking things too fast.

"Well not exactly *met*. I inadvertently overheard your name being mentioned." She was in dangerous water now. "Er, well, I assumed it was your name . . ."

"How fascinating."

"Do you know a woman called Vlasta?"

"I once knew a woman who calls herself Vlasta, Vlasta Balkova. She thinks she's a Russian concert pianist. God only knows why. Her piano-playing is atrocious. Where did you come across her?"

"Oh, just bumped into her . . ."

"She lets out rooms. If you're desperate, I could take you there."

"Thanks, but no thanks."

"I stayed in her house for a while when I first came to London. Her piano practice drove me out. I'm a music lover. They say practice makes perfect, yet in Vlasta's case the reverse was true." Rainey looked thoughtful. "What did she say about me? What did you overhear?"

"It was nothing really. She and her girlfriend were having a row on the bus."

"Jesus, you mean my name was being bandied about on public transport!"

Madeline was mortified. "Oh God, I'm really sorry. I shouldn't have mentioned it. Can we talk about something else? Vlasta gives me the creeps."

"OK. Have you ever been fucked in the back of a Rolls Royce?"

Madeline choked. "Never, but I did it in the back of a post office van in Yorkshire once. I've still got the imprint of the spare tyre on my backside. I've never even ridden in a Rolls Royce."

"I happen to have one outside," Rainey said. "Shall we go?"

chapter 10

Why was everyone so high? Ruby, Cynthia, Herbert, Rose, Mary and Reen: they'd all been locked out that morning. Perhaps it was the fantastically beautiful sunrise. Herbert marched straight into the kitchen and began frying bacon and eggs. Reen made a jug of coffee. Ruby, Rose, Cynthia and Mary sat in a row on the sofa in the front room with their feet up and let themselves be waited on.

For the first time, Mary was at Reen's house. It was nothing like she had imagined. She assumed all her workmates lived in the same small boxes on estates, but this was a real, solid house with a heavy wooden staircase going straight up from the front door and a hallway through to the kitchen at the back. The rooms were a decent size, the shelves stuffed with books and papers. Untidy.

"I like your house," she said. "It's kind of homey."

"It was better before all the posers moved into the street," Reen said. "They've gutted the insides and put in spiral stairs and fancy kitchens. This is the only original house left."

"Your kitchen is what I call well-stocked." Herbert said, balancing plates of food. "Good sharp knives and all the herbs and spices." Reen went pink, Mary noticed.

"What time's the post?" Cynthia asked.

"About 8.30. Hours yet . . ."

The very thing Mary had lain awake at night worrying about had come to pass. No job. And here she was calmly drinking coffee with her feet up as if she didn't have a care in the world.

After the fry-up, they went out into the narrow garden and smoked home-grown.

She couldn't remember ever enjoying such companionship. Although she didn't talk much, she didn't feel left out. What could she say? Life had always been dull. She craved more.

Herbert told them he used to be a butcher. Had a stall in Ridley Road. "I went down Smithfield five o'clock every mornin' to buy me meat, the only black person in the place. It was full of national fronts and Powellites. Remember that man? Rivers of blood? I saw rivers of blood down that place. I nearly shit meself when I see all them carcases hanging up on big hooks. I thought my ass will end up on one of them."

"You were crazy, man, going down there!" Cynthia exclaimed.

"What happened?" Ruby wanted to know. "What happened to your stall?"

"Went bankrupt. All me friends come along and load up with lumps o' meat. Pay you next week, they said, pay you on pay day. No-one paid. But we had great parties with plenty o' goat and lamb curry."

"I'd of gone vegetarian," Cynthia said and they laughed till it hurt.

"What's your dear husband going to say when you get home?" Reen asked, turning to Mary.

"He hardly ever opens his gob, so it will be a big deal if he says anything at all," she replied.

"I still feel shit about me fox's paw the other day," Ruby giggled and then the whole story of Mary's husband, the union man, was recounted to Herbert. They all started laughing again and this time they couldn't stop. Mary rolled on the ground clinging to her stomach.

A window crashed open above their heads and an annoyed voice called out:

"Ma! What's going on, I'm trying to sleep." Mary looked up and glimpsed a young black man in a flapping white night shirt. Then the sash window slammed down.

"Bloody cheek," Reen said.

"Don't call the boy names," said Ruby. "You know you're damn proud. Handsome and clever."

"You'll soon be a grandmother," teased Herbert.

"Don't count on it," Reen said, "it can't happen stuck in his room day and night in front of that screen."

"He'll do his eyes in," Cynthia observed and added casually, "where's the dad?"

Mary was shocked by Cynthia's directness.

"Went back to the Caribbean years ago. Too much sense to hang around here," said Reen.

"Sense got nothing to do with it," Cynthia frowned. "You get responsibilities. You get stuck."

"Well," said Herbert, standing up. "I better not get stuck here." He took Reen's telephone number and promised to call to consult before the meeting.

"Try to get hold of as many of the others as you can. Persuade them to come," Reen pleaded.

"I better get going too," Mary said sleepily but didn't move. Was it a school day? She couldn't remember. In any case, Terry was home and could see to the kids.

Reen dozed with her chin on her chest. Cynthia was sprawled in a canvas deck chair and Ruby had gone inside to lie down.

So Reen had a grown son. That made her older than Mary. Much older. Maybe forty. She didn't really know fuck-all about Reen. It was disappointing because her plan that she and Reen should become best friends might not work with Reen being much older. It was too unequal.

It was clear to her now that the bad vibes between Reen and Nell had to do with Reen having a black son, even though it was never talked about at work. Or maybe it had been? Maybe she had blanked it out like she did when Terry made his comments? Always steering the conversation away, never challenging it.

"Reen!" she said, "did I tell you about the file I found?"

"What?"

"A few weeks ago. I found a file in the directors' dining room and I took it home."

Reen opened one eye. "What's it about?"

"Don't know, do I? I'm not much of a one for reading," Mary replied sulkily. "In strict confidence, it said, strict confidence. That's why I took it."

The window flew up again. "Mum, the bloody doorbell!"

Slam!

"I'm going to break that boy's bleedin' neck one of these days!" Reen fumed. "Lazy little bastard!"

She got up with an angry expression and went inside.

Mary's eyelids were like lead and her eyeballs felt like hard-boiled eggs. Her mouth was dry as a vulture's crotch. Cynthia was snoring, a blissed-out expression on her face. Mary rolled over and got on all fours. From that position she managed to launch herself to her feet and drag herself indoors. It was hot in the house. A postman was at the front door and Reen was sitting on the bottom of the stairs, signing for something.

"This is it," she told Mary. "Get Cynthia in here."

They gathered in the front room. "It's like waiting for a will to be read," Ruby said, sitting primly.

Reen put on her glasses.

"OK. Listen to this: 'We regret to inform you that due to the serious contraction of the news industry and the centralization and computerization of news gathering, we have negotiated with your trade union a reduction of fifty jobs. In return the company has agreed to recognize your Union as the sole representative of the staff in its employ.'"

"Well, that's nice!"

"Shut up!"

Reen read on, " 'We are still in discussion with the union regarding the terms of redundancy, however this will not be less than two weeks' pay for every year of service.' "

They all stared at each other. Cynthia was the first to break the silence. "I told you that fuckin' woman sold us out!"

"I'm not sure if she knew anything about it," Mary said timidly. They looked at her as if she'd come down in the last shower.

"Why did she run like hell when she see all of we this morning?" Cynthia said forcefully. "She knew straight away what's happening."

"If Jack's a scab, Terry's a feckin' scab too. So how comes Nell knows what's going on, and I don't?" Mary cried desperately.

"Because Nell's the Mother of the Chapel, the two of them work together, mister and missus, that's how," Reen said.

"I thought Jack was a decent feller. Him and his ethics," Mary admitted. "I knew he was mean but I thought he had ethics."

"You can't be mean *and* ethical," Reen said. "Anyway, what does it matter? You always get this where there's couples working together and there's industrial action. There's always one pair that splits up. The husband goes one way and the wife goes the other. Remember Lil, Rubes? She bashed her old man over the head with a banner pole when he tried to cross the picket line at *The Times*."

"Did they ever get back together?" Mary asked.

"Are you serious?"

"They didn't?"

"Of course they bloody didn't. She done six months in Holloway. He went and shacked up with his bit on the side."

"Forget all that," Ruby said, and squeezed Mary's arm. "Don't get upset about it love. Everyone understands. We're all

in the same boat. So let's just think what to do about our jobs."
They knitted their brows. "Someone should find out what the
union head office got to say about this," suggested Cynthia.

"We should make placards and a banner," said Ruby. "Get a
picket line going. Remember that time we threw that pin-stripe
berk in the river, Reen? Took off his trousers and threw him in
the river?"

"How could I forget?"

"And one time we beat up a scab with our umbrellas," Ruby
hooted.

"What was that about?" Mary asked. "Wapping, of course,"
said Ruby.

"Why are you always going on about it? You lost it didn't
you?"

"Listen girlie, don't get shirty just because we've forgotten
stuff that you never knew. You win some, you lose some. You'll
learn," Reen said. "Why don't you run along home and see if
you can get anything out of Nellie. Act friendly. Have a peek in
your ole man's fancy briefcase, maybe there's more in there
than sandwiches. Get that file you been going on about. Ruby,
you get down to head office and see if you can prise any sense out
of the buggers. Cynthia and I will make placards. We can't make
a banner till we've had a meeting and agreed what to put on it.

"Anyone you can think of contacting to come to the
meeting, do it, whether they're in the same union or not. We
need a big turn-out if we're going to build up a campaign. We've
got to put maximum pressure on these bastards."

"Where's your loo," Mary sniffed. It was well past her
bedtime. Things were moving too fast. How was she going to
stay awake till five o'clock and then attend a meeting? From the
sound of things, Reen and the others had in mind picketing the
building. When were they ever going to get any rest?

.

It was just before noon when she put the key in the lock. The flat was quiet. First she thought there was no-one in. Then she saw Terry in his new tee shirt and jeans. His papers were spread out all over the kitchen table.

"Where the hell was you this morning?" he glared.

"We all got feckin' locked out, Terry. Do you know anything about it?" The little shite didn't even try to cover up or apologize. Didn't hesitate. It was like he was proud of it.

"We had to," he said sullenly. "They told us the first union to give them a list of fifty names for the chop would get sole recognition." Then he noticed her face. "What are you up tight about? You don't have to work. You got them kids to look after. And I'll be earning a lot more. I'm management now."

"Not round here, you're not, mate," she said with loathing.

"What do you mean? You're getting weirder and weirder you are," he said, shaking his head and laughing nervously.

"What about all them poor bastards who joined the union for support? What happens to them? What happens to all them other unions now the bosses don't recognize them?"

"You always said there should be one union for the print."

"Don't play the smart arse with me, Terry. You've made me look a feckin' scab, being married to one and having another two for neighbours. How many names did Nell give you to make up the fifty? Was my name on the list? Was I one of the fifty?"

"If we didn't co-operate, the paper would of closed and we'd all of been out of a job."

"What a disaster, no more tits and bums. No more jobs for the boys!"

Her eye caught an unfamiliar object which sat on top of the fridge next to the phone. A flat box with two slits in front. It wasn't there before.

"What's that? A new toaster?"

"It's a fax you silly cow. Me and Jack have been faxing the

crap out of each other all morning!"

"You could have fooled me," she said.

Terry snickered, trying to give the impression he understood her insult.

"Where is he?"

"Who? Jack? Down the pub."

"You mean he's faxing from the pub? Just over the road?"

"Yeah, so what?"

"You're pathetic. Both of you," she said. "Look, I don't want a row now. I'm knackered. I'm going to crash out for a couple of hours. When the kids come in, get them a snack. There's salad and cheese in the fridge. And for Christ's sake, whatever you do, don't give them tap water."

She dreamt of Patrice and Reen who were merged into one. An idyllic place by a river. Picnics. Laughing with friends. Feeling randy. And all this happening in another country.

Loud knocking put an end to it. Jack shouting through the letter box. "Tel, Tel! Quick!" Then she heard their low voices in the kitchen. Fuckin' cow this, fuckin' cow that.

"I'll ask her," Terry said. Next minute he appeared in the doorway, his face even more rigid than usual.

"Nell's disappeared," he whispered. Mary couldn't understand why they were so upset. "Have you seen her?" he asked agitatedly.

Mary tried to think. It was light years ago.

"I saw her at the bus stop last night on me way to work. As soon as she saw the lock-out she turned round and went home."

"And you haven't seen her since?"

"No. God, I hope she's all right. Hasn't she been home?"

She dragged herself out of bed and pulled on her clothes. "Has Jack phoned all the places she might have gone?"

Terry didn't answer. He was already in the kitchen conveying her reply. Jack didn't look up or respond to her greeting. He was sitting at the table with his face in his hands. "Put the kettle on," Terry ordered.

Tears dribbled between Jack's fingers. She was gob-smacked. She had no idea they were so close.

When the tea was ready she patted his shoulder as she put the cup down in front of him. "Don't worry, love," she murmured, "Nellie can look after herself. She'll turn up."

He leapt up and banged his fist on the table. "I don't give a stuff whether she turns up or not," he shouted. "I want my fuckin' money back!"

"She's taken his money," Terry said accusingly. "Grands in cash. She could be half-way to Australia by now."

Mary's jaw dropped.

"She's a brother in New Zealand," she blurted out, and Jack fell back and began blubbering. Terry gave her a furious look.

"Let's go to yours and see if we can find any clues," Terry said importantly and Mary tagged along, concealing her utter glee. Wait till Reen and the others heard about this!

A metal cash box lay gaping and empty on the draining board by the sink. The freezer door was hanging open.

"Look at this," Mary exclaimed. She pulled out some of the frozen packets of food. "They're all labelled. Christ, she must have been cooking for weeks." Each meal was tagged with the contents and the date to be consumed: tea, Friday 17th November; dinner, Friday 17th November; breakfast, Saturday 18th November; and so on. Mary rummaged till she found Christmas dinner. "She must have planned this well in advance. Well in advance."

"Shut up, bitch," Terry hissed, "you're only upsetting him."

"No. Think, Terry. Remember when she went to her mother's funeral? She did the same then. Cooked up loads of meals for Jack and labelled them all. Maybe this means she'll be back after Christmas?"

Jack sobbed.

"Well, I must love you and leave you," Mary said breezily. "I've a meeting to get to. Oh, Terry, when the kids come in, don't forget to put the super-lice gel on their hair? It has to be done every day without fail."

She went back to their own flat and took a quick shower. Much as she disliked Nell, she had to hand it to her this time. Half-way to New Zealand! Jesus Christ! She wondered if travel would broaden the rotten cow's mind. When she came out of the bathroom, Terry was still not back. She was on her way out the door when she remembered the file.

chapter 11

When Rosemary thought about it afterwards, she realized her attendance at Wimbledon was bound to attract the prurient attention of the gutter press. Certain elements among the women players had given the tournament a bad name. In hindsight it was so obvious. It was galling that poor Helen's name had been dragged into it. And she had been such a good friend recently! All this added extra urgency to the early announcement of Rosemary's impending nuptials. There was only one impediment. She had not yet met and approved the intended groom.

All she knew was that he was a fellow officer of Helen's husband, Roger. They had met while serving on the Royal yacht. Like Rosemary, he preferred celibacy and, according to Helen, was a reserved person with great depth of character. He simply wasn't interested in women. Not in "that way".

Now that the pressure was about to be lifted, Rosemary found it easier to talk more frankly to Helen. It had become less and less obligatory to keep re-stating her denial. And Helen was the perfect friend, simpatico and loyal. The misunderstandings of the past were behind them.

Yes, life was easier. Even Celeste was subdued. Rosemary had told her a little white lie. She had been led to believe her dear pussy had died on the operating table. Thank heavens, she had not insisted on viewing the remains. The truth was, Pud was alive and well at the cat sanctuary in Cambridgeshire. Rosemary had no need to feel even the slightest twinge of guilt. On the contrary, she congratulated herself on having disposed of the nuisance so propitiously. For she had been amazed and delighted when, on arrival at the sanctuary, she found rows of gaily painted miniature chalets for the cats and dogs. Pud was received with open arms.

"Come here, darling!" cooed the receptionist as she lifted Pud out of her basket. Rosemary was handed forms which were the feline equivalent of adoption papers. Henceforth she was pledged to renounce all interest in the animal. She signed with alacrity. So great was her relief, she impetuously added an extra nought when she wrote out a cheque for the obligatory donation.

Daddy had converted the attic into a music room. Not personally of course: a tradesman did the manual work. Everything was planned meticulously but, in the pre-eminent, final plan, he never lived to see his project completed. The acoustics were wonderfully fine and Rosemary went up there in the evenings to listen to music: Poulenc's Clarinet Sonata, the Solo Clarinet Suite by Stravinsky, and her very favourite, The Serious Doll by Elgar. These sounds suited her ear, affirmed her solitariness and detachment. Or, when she was in a cool, mathematical mood she enjoyed Glenn Gould's Goldberg Variations. The notes drummed on her tight skull inducing a state of private feeling which, she reluctantly admitted to herself, was nothing but a form of masturbation. The romantic composers were far too disturbing. The guitar playing of Segovia thrilled her romantically but not unbearably. It was romanticism in miniaturized form.

Once, while still at school, she had felt romantic about an older girl, a prefect who had startlingly blue eyes. Nothing carnal, only heart fluttering, innocent blushes, the sort of feelings girls were supposed to grow out of, she supposed. Late for games one day, she found the locker room empty, save for rows of blazers and gym slips hanging on pegs. Pinned to the beloved one's lapel was a yellow jonquil. Rosemary stood on tip-toe and sniffed the flower, experiencing a moment of sublime, naive ecstasy. For some time she cherished this memory, until the guileless sweetness evaporated and was, by and by, replaced by fear, shame and denial. She had not thought of it for years, until the day in Sir Gregory's office when the fear and self-loathing returned.

It was Helen who had seen her through, stood by her and restored her. As a gesture of trust and friendship, Rosemary had agreed they would go to Greece together as soon as the marriage arrangements had been finalized.

After listening to her music one evening, Rosemary found Celeste nibbling a snack in the kitchen.

"What's that cheap, horrible smell?" Rosemary complained. She hated perfume. To her it reeked of overt sexuality: civets' cervixes. Her mother wore Schiaparelli and Balenciaga. It was disgusting. She was an old woman!

"Helen rang for you," Celeste said between mouthfuls.

"When? Why didn't you call me?"

"I did," Celeste said. "You were incommunicado as usual. You had those damn headphones on. And, for your information, my lady, in India, even the men anoint their bodies with fragrant oils. There's nothing odd or cheap about it. In fact, it's good for the soul."

"Damn. It's too late to ring her now," Rosemary said distractedly.

Next morning, Sunday, she waited until nine o'clock to ring Helen. By then, she judged her friend would be up and doing. But Helen sounded testy.

"I rang last night to make a date for you to meet Gresby."

Rosemary was a bag of nerves. "I don't know if I can go ahead with this," she said, speaking quietly. Celeste hovered nearby.

"Oh, for God's sake, Rosemary, people do it all the time," Helen said in a tight, annoyed voice.

"All right, you pick the time and place. Whatever suits you."

"Are you crazy? I'm not going to be there. You *are* a funny old thing, Rosemary!" Helen groaned.

Rosemary was silent. Helen was not going to be there to support her when she met this strange man. "Are you listening?" her friend went on, "He's given me a string of dates. You can choose one that suits you." Rosemary automatically picked up a pencil and wrote them down.

"I'll call you back," she said dully, replacing the receiver.

Celeste darted to her side. "What's happening?"

"Mind your own business, Mother. What are you doing out of bed?"

"What's going to happen to me when you get married?" Celeste wailed. "Are you going to have me put down, as you did poor Pud?"

"Nothing is going to change, Mother, have you got that? Nothing! The only change will be that I won't have to put up with innuendos and harassment any more. Get it?"

"A marriage of convenience?"

"Let us hope so," Rosemary replied.

"I know everything there is to know about marriages of convenience," Celeste said inexplicably. But Rosemary took no notice. She had begun to steel herself for the drive down to Portsmouth for the meeting with Gresby, which was to take place at a hotel. They were to dine together; then she would stay over at Helen's and drive back to London next morning.

Gresby was four inches taller than Rosemary, slim, long-legged, and handsome-faced. Thick, blond hair sprouted from a widow's peak although his eyebrows were amazingly black. His skin was smooth and tanned. His perfect teeth formed a wonderful smile. His clothes were divine. Rosemary was quite astonished. She had dressed down, in a sombre suit with pearls. He wore a short-waisted cream jacket which crossed over and buttoned up somewhere under his right armpit, with a soft leather belt and loosely tailored trousers.

As they ascended the stairway of the Imperial Hotel on their way to dinner Rosemary noticed him pause for a split second to look at himself in the ornamental mirror. Her hand was on top of his forearm in the old-fashioned way and she felt uneasy when he said: "We make a splendid couple," in a satisfied tone. She hoped there was no misunderstanding. Surely she could trust Helen to get it right? Gresby lingered on the threshold as they were about to enter the dining room and smiled, long and hard. Several flashes occurred before Rosemary realized they were being photographed.

"Our whole game plan depends on maximum exposure, right?" he said. As they followed the waiter across an expanse of shimmering ballroom to reach their table, Rosemary detached herself from Gresby's arm in case the band struck up and she might be trapped into dancing. Half way across she felt dizzy and would have stumbled had not the alert and attentive Gresby once more gallantly proffered his arm. At that precise moment she was filled with an unaccountable sense of déjà vu.

Watching him eat she realized he was considerably younger than herself. Helen had failed to inform her of this.

"I've heard a lot about your father," he said out of the blue. "What a tragic loss!"

"I was very young," Rosemary offered. Seventeen was not so very young but it was none of Gresby's business.

"Apparently he had a reputation as a strict disciplinarian," Gresby said unctuously.

"I wouldn't know anything about that," Rosemary replied sternly. She never talked about her father. They ate in silence. Gresby emptied his glass several times. Rosemary had fathomed her strange feeling of having been there before. It was not déjà vu. It was history repeating itself. She felt she was playing Celeste's role and Gresby was standing in for her father. Why this ghostly illusion had come to her she did not know. And she did not want to know.

Yes. Celeste would have been in her element. The ostentation, the colonial trappings. There were even ceiling fans gently stirring the air. "All we need is a punkahwalla," Rosemary thought.

Gresby ordered more wine but she placed her hand over her glass.

"I'm driving. And I'm not familiar with this part of the world."

"Obviously not," Gresby said smarmily. A twitch started up in the corner of his mouth.

"Did you know that a word-processor can be programmed to make tiny differences, perhaps in word spacing, that would make it easy to trace a leak to a limited number in a department or even to a single person?"

Rosemary did not like this topic either. She had not gone along with this charade to talk about her father or her "case". As far as she was concerned the evening was a formality. Now their pictures had been taken they could both go home. But Gresby, it seemed, wanted to talk. "You can have no idea what a privilege, what a rare treat it is for me, to be sitting here like this with you," he said. "You're such a good listener. Usually, I'm tongue-tied in the company of women." He poured himself more wine.

Rosemary tried to interrupt. She wanted to say: there is no need to ingratiate yourself. Not only is it cringe-making but it is entirely pointless. Her gaze kept straying to his hairline. His black roots alarmed her.

"I haven't got any women friends," he continued, his speech affected by the alcohol. "You are the only sort of woman I could possibly bear to sit near . . . like this . . . talking with."

"This too will pass," Rosemary told herself, counting her breathing.

"You don't know what it's like for me," Gresby went on, clenching his knuckles, an ivory pallor visible beneath the tan. "Everywhere I turn I feel women pressing in on me, bursting out of the television with their tits on display. Even standing on the escalator in the underground, driving on the motorway, everywhere you look, there are hoardings with naked women thrusting out, suffocating me. White-titted whores!"

Rosemary sat in silence waiting for it to end.

How she drove back to Helen's she could not remember. She fell in through Helen's front door. Dinner with Gresby had reduced her to a rag doll.

"Helen," she cried to her friend, "the man is unbalanced!"

"What do you mean?"

"He hates women!"

"Don't they all?" Helen said blandly.

Rosemary broke down. "Not my daddy," she sobbed. "Not my daddy."

She could never have explained to Helen the peculiar feelings she had experienced in the company of Gresby. She did not understand them herself and that made her frightened. It was impossible to be angry with Helen, even though she felt let down. Helen had failed to notice that Gresby was a madman. Helen had failed to protect her from his madness: had even promoted the idea of them marrying!

They were sitting side by side on the plump sofa in Helen's cosy front room. Helen held Rosemary's head and dabbed at her eyes with a tissue. The curtains were drawn and a small portable air conditioner hummed in the fireplace.

"Tell me all about it," Helen said softly. After her cry, Rosemary was calm. She began to talk.

"I've forgotten my entire childhood," she said. "I can't remember anything. All I can remember is sniffing a flower on another girl's blazer at school. I remember when daddy was awarded the OBE and telling other girls about it. Bragging. But their fathers all had CBEs or titles. I've always thought close relationships were unhealthy . . ."

"I know," Helen said, "I've heard you use the word 'unhealthy' more than once and I've always wondered what you meant by it. What do you mean?"

"I can't explain . . ." Somehow her head had come to rest on Helen's lap. It was a delicious sensation and quite legitimate. She was entitled to receive the comfort of a friend. In any case, she was too tired to move. "I've never had a friend. You're the only one. I've never talked to anyone." Tears rolled down her cheeks and Helen dabbed some more, her upside-down face close. Distorted. Rosemary felt oppressed. Her body leaden; overcome by tiredness.

"Let's get you to bed," Helen said.

There was no evidence of Roger in the house.

Celeste was beside herself when she saw the pictures of Rosemary and Gresby. "I must meet him, I *must*!" She was like a mewling child. Confronted with Rosemary's obdurate silence she cried: "If you let me meet him, I'll forgive you for murdering Pud!"

Rosemary had to smile. It was on the tip of her tongue to tell her mother the cat was alive and well at the cat sanctuary.

Better judgement told her that if Celeste ever found out Pud's whereabouts she would be sure to go there and return with not just one cat but several.

chapter 12

"What I like about Kitty's," Rainey called as she plied the wheel, "is you've got women of all ages, sizes, nationalities, colours . . . together, all in one room, all getting on fine with each other, know what I mean?"

"Sort of," Madeline said, not wishing to contradict her new friend. They were speeding north, Madeline in the back seat, luxuriating in the upholstery. Rainey wore her chauffeur's cap and fingerless driving gloves. They kept catching each other's eye in the rear view mirror. Madeline almost remembered how it was to be shy.

"Open the cabinet in front of you and help yourself to a drink," Rainey said, and Madeline poured a ready-mixed Southern Comfort into a paper cup. Rainey waved at a street as they sped by. "I once had a relationship with a woman who lived in that street," she said.

"Where are we? I don't know this part of London."

Rainey didn't answer till they'd negotiated a roundabout. "I'm taking you up to Ally Pally, then we'll come back around the top of Hampstead Heath."

They were climbing. Madeline saw the lights of the city twinkling in the mauve sky. "It's gorgeous."

"See that street," Rainey pointed again, "I had a relationship with a woman who lived there."

"Why don't you just point out the streets where you *didn't*."

Rainey smiled and the car bowled along in silence for a while.

"Tell me about the lesbian civil servant?" Madeline asked. "Did you ever drive her?"

"Of course, frequently. I picked her up from Victoria Station every morning. You are sitting in the very spot where she sat. Can you feel her vibes?"

"No." The back of Lorraine's neck looked delectable from that angle, wisps of blonde hair showing under the cap. Rosemary must have been creaming her knickers. Maddy remembered how Carol hated that expression.

"And Sir Gregory was her boss?" she persevered.

"Right. Do you want to get in the front now?" Rainey said, slowing the car.

"Yes please."

They stopped and Madeline clambered out and got into the front seat. The car door shut with a sound like gold bars clunking together.

"What did you make of her? Is she a dyke?"

As the car floated away from the kerb, Rainey answered. "The bitch is so fucking tense, she can't enjoy the luxurious life she lives. I'm not one of those who resents people having a bit of dosh. I love to see people spending money when they're not used to having it. They can enjoy it, you know, really savour it. Foreign holidays, good food and all that. But that tight-assed female was born to it and doesn't know she's alive."

"So you didn't like her . . ."

"Didn't like her vibes."

"What does she look like? The pictures are always blurred."

"Nice legs, quite tall, thick brownish hair. Square-jawed, teeth like dice, pugnacious looking, not much make-up, expensive jewellery, nice legs, oh I said that already? Oozes money, money, money. Supercilious expression."

"I think she was fitted up with the leak," Madeline said tentatively.

"You're quick!" Rainey was sarcastic. "It's common knowledge."

Madeline was stung. She liked to think she was always one step ahead of the game. Her mind raced. "Common among whom?" she said.

"Us commoners," Rainey retorted flippantly, then dropped the subject. "You know they ask me to put the glass partition across when they want to talk privately? They think I can't hear, but I can. One time I heard them discussing some poor bastard, or, more likely, a rich bastard, who'd applied for a job.

"Sir Gregory said he'd turned him down because he was a Quaker. The other guy in the back couldn't believe it, 'Not Rodney! A Quaker. Surely not . . .'

"Sir Gregory said 'Oh well, he may not exactly be a Quaker, but he's definitely suspect. He's the kind of person who's kind to lesbian mothers and asylum-seekers, so he wouldn't fit in here.' "

Madeline feigned a yawn. Rainey's attractiveness had receded. Whole sentences came back to her from an article she had read in a civil service journal. "It is common knowledge that Government Ministers use the technique of leaking sensitive proposals on certain legislation in advance. They leak the proposals to the media and in that way it is not too late to adjust intended legislation according to the way the public reacts. It is common practice."

"I'm tired," she said in a tense voice, "can you drop me?" They were in the Euston Road.

"At your service, ma'am," Rainey said. Sweet little dimples appeared at the corners of her mouth and she touched her cap in a pretend salute. Madeline was not about to be won over by such a blatant display of cuteness but her pique began to dissolve.

"Anywhere round Holborn will do," she said. She had in

mind calling at the paper, talking to Gordon, then getting him to book her a taxi on his expense account.

"Going to the newspaper office?" Rainey asked and again Madeline was peeved by her over-smartness. Without waiting for an answer, Rainey said: "The car's a bit conspicuous so I'll drop you round the corner."

They drew up at the top of Gray's Inn Road and Madeline got out. "Thanks for the ride," she said, looking at Rainey for some sign. "That's OK," Rainey was suddenly brisk. She picked up a card from the dashboard and handed it to Madeline. "That's my number. If you're stuck for somewhere to stay I can fix you up at Vlasta's."

"Thanks," Madeline said wryly. She clunked the door and the car rolled away.

There was no-one about and the street lights were filtered throught a dirty, yellow heat haze. Her footsteps rang on the pavement in a girlie way as she walked. She was not used to heels. Rainey had depressed her by belittling the lesbian mole story, and she felt bitterly disappointed with herself. She blamed Carol. Carol had dulled her wits with her cuddly toys and baby talk. But did she really want an equal, adult relationship? Could she handle it? Or did she always have to be in control? Even though she'd spontaneously enjoyed most of the evening, at the end of it she felt she'd come off second best in her encounter with Rainey.

Then, in the distance she saw a man she thought was Colin Shadbolt coming towards her. Not wishing to speak to him in such a deserted place, she hurriedly crossed the road with her eyes down. When she looked up again the street was empty. It was spooky. She thought maybe he had disappeared down a side alley but it was empty. She remembered, long ago, walking from Blackfriars Station towards Fleet Street in a winter afternoon drizzle, seeing Shadbolt emerge from the golf shop that used to be on Bridge Street. She had recognized his shiny face as he aggressively hoisted up his big new umbrella. He must have heard her laughter as it collapsed slowly about his head and she dated his vendetta against her from that moment. She had been in the wrong place at the wrong time. The story of her life.

She cut through Shoe Lane hoping to find a caff open in the alley where lorries with massive, scary wheels once carried rolls of newsprint to feed the presses of the *Express* and *Standard*. But nothing moved. The *Telegraph* clock, titivated for the tourists who still came to Fleet Street, told her it was now 6 am. When she turned the corner she was surprised to see several people, one of whom was Gordon, forming a straggly picket line outside the building. As she approached them she suppressed a satisfied smirk. None of them had supported her when she was sacked. Gordon looked shabby and downtrodden. Just as she was about to speak to him, Shadbolt stepped in front of her.

"What are you doing here, Silver?" he said pleasantly.

Instinctively Madeline shouted: "I've come here to tell you I'm sueing your arse for wrongful dismissal!"

He spat his cigar butt onto the pavement. "Wake up, lady," he sneered. "What year do you think you're living in? Look at this bunch of losers," he said, indicating Gordon and the others.

"There are international laws!"

"Yeah? Who's going to implement them, a UN task force?" he guffawed. Then he quickly became serious, sincere. He laid one hand on her shoulder. "Tell you what, Silver," he said in a low confidential voice, walking her a few steps away from the curious picketers. "I'm willing to talk to you. If I can persuade the powers that be to have you back . . . we'll see. I make no promises, but come and see me at ten this morning and we'll talk." Then he disappeared through the swing doors.

She was dumbfounded. Gordon shuffled over with an

inquisitive expression. "You gave him an earful, what did he say?"

"Nothing. The usual garbage," Madeline replied, trying to cover her confusion. "What happened to you?" she asked Gordon. "How come you're out here? Who's left inside who knows how to put a paper together?"

He shrugged. "No-one I know of, but who cares? That's not the object of the exercise any more. The paper's just a public relations sheet for Japanese interests . . ." While Gordon expounded his theory, Madeline's mind was occupied with how she was going to fill up the next few hours until ten o'clock.

"I was relying on you, Gordon," she said. "I wanted you to fix me up with a cab on exes." His drooping shoulders twitched. "Why not book in to Bloomsburys? Charge it up to the paper," he suggested.

"Do you think it would work?"

chapter 13

After freshening up at the hotel, Madeline felt like a new woman. "Feeling like a new woman" was one of the coupley little jokes she and Carol indulged in together.

She arrived back outside the building at ten. At a guess there were about fifty men and women milling around. Half a dozen police were trying to get them to spread out along the footpath, jostling them over towards the side of the building.

Above the hubbub an emaciated youth chanted "Work for the return of a radical Labour Government!" What does it mean? Maddy thought, have I missed something? There were the usual Trot paper-sellers. "How many SWP members does it take to sell a paper to a crowd of fifty?" she muttered as she pushed her way through. One of them elbowed her viciously in the ribs and hissed in her ear, "It's slags like you who divide the working class."

Mary, the Irish cleaner, was shyly handing out leaflets. Madeline took one. "You too? Is anybody left in there?"

"We're having meetings," Mary said, "those of us who've been sacked. You're welcome to come along. Reen's organizing it."

"What happened to Nell?"

"We don't know. We think she done a runner. Might have gone to New Zealand."

Madeline didn't know what to make of this information. She shook her head, frowning as she skimmed the hand-out.

"I can't make five today but I'd like to get involved." She pointed to the phone number on the bottom of the leaflet. "Is this Reen's number?" Mary nodded. "Tell her I'll give her a ring. Oh, by the way . . ." Just in time, she covered up a patronizing wink. That's what growing up is all about, she thought. Almost behaving like a jerk but managing to stop yourself just in time.

"I've got your address," she said, "and I've been wanting to speak to you."

The little cleaner looked stunned: "You've got my feckin' address? How the jesus fuck did you get it?"

"We journalists have our ways," Madeline said tapping the side of her nose as she pressed onwards.

"What a feckin' cheek!" Mary exploded behind her back. Madeline didn't catch her exact words.

"Where do you think you're going?" The Commissionaire barred her way as she tried to enter the swing doors.

"I've got an appointment with Mr Shadbolt at ten," Madeline whispered.

He checked his clip-board, "Name?" "Silver." He ticked her name on a list and she was through. Inside she was confronted with computerized gates into which authorized persons inserted a plastic key-card to gain entry. She had no card. Hers had been demanded back when she left. It was like getting your cards in reverse, because when you got the sack you had to hand over your entry card to security before they let you out of the building for the last time.

A uniformed man sitting in a glass box on the other side pressed a button, released one of the gates, and waved her through.

"Is that cage bullet proof?" she joked, but apparently he wasn't amused. "Humourless git," she muttered.

This was a computerized lock-out. Nullify the cards selectively after your employees have left the building and you don't even have to lock the doors to stop them getting back in. They get the news they're sacked when the machine spits out their card. She summoned the lift. Down the social you get another bit of plastic to use in shops. They put it in the till like a credit card and read off your entitlement. Not valid for alcohol or tobacco. Madeline had been learning the bullfuckshit hard way.

She stepped out of the lift and looked around. The low hum of the machines was the only sound. There was no sign of paper. Two gormless teenage boys sat at the desk she and Gordon used to share. Nobody she knew. When they saw her they giggled and nudged each other.

Shadbolt's secretary appeared. "This way, Miz Silver," she said, exchanging glances with the boys.

The editor was reclining in his old leather chair with his heels on the desk as usual.

"Seriously Miz Silver, I mean this sincerely. I'm glad you've turned up. I've been ringing round but nobody seemed to know where you were. All I got was an Ansaphone or a string of abuse from that mad bitch you used to live with."

"You've been ringing me?"

"Indeed I have," he said cordially. "We've got a special job for you. Made for you. Of course you won't be on the payroll. That's for plebs. You'll have your own individual contract . . ."

"Which you can tear up any time you feel like . . ."

"Now, now. Don't be like that. At least hear me out."

"What is this mysterious job?"

"Remember the Lesbian Mole story?"

"How could I forget it? A plant if ever there was one. Why would an upper-class dyke come running to this grubby little rag and ask Colin Shadbolt the well-known queer-basher to tell her story?"

"See? I knew you were the right woman for the job. What with being acey-dicey yourself" (he made a gesture with one hand), "you'll be right in there like a rat up a drainpipe."

His secretary put her head round the door. "Not now Julie, Miz Silver and I are in conference. Hold all calls."

"I am *not* acey-dicey!"

"Look at this," he rummaged on his desk and pushed a cutting over. "Nice clear picture," Madeline commented. It was Rosemary on the arm of a blond hunk.

"Now *that's* what I call phoney," Shadbolt said with a hideous grin. Madeline knew what he meant but didn't let it show.

"Are you worried that this announcement makes your so-called exclusive look rather foolish?" Madeline asked calmly.

"Not at all. Because we are going to show the public the truth, the whole truth and nothing but the truth," Shadbolt said indignantly. Madeline was always intrigued when he simulated the behaviour of an ethical journalist with the public interest at heart.

"Pull the other one," she said.

"We are not interested only in Rosemary now. The boyfriend is also of considerable interest to us. A very juicy story there. Very juicy." As if to emphasize the importance of what he was about to divulge, he removed his feet from the desk, leaned forward and mouthed portentously. "He has worked on the Royal Yacht!"

"Do you want me to spy through his port-hole?" Madeline quipped.

Shadbolt was offended. "Are you interested or not?"

"It's all very fascinating," Madeline said, "but I don't see any work in it for me."

"We've done a lot of research," Shadbolt said. "We've found out all sorts of stuff about Rosemary's mummy and daddy and their hijinks in foreign parts. Look at this . . ." He opened his desk drawer and pulled out a dilapidated old library file.

Madeline was surprised. "I thought all the library stuff was on microfile now?"

"Not everything," Shadbolt said. "We don't want *everything* accessible, do we?"

She opened the bundle of cuttings and sifted through. "These are ancient," she said.

"Diplomat Slain". "Shots Ring Out Under Cover of Independence Celebrations", the headline said.

"Is that her father?"

"You can take that with you. Read it later. I just wanted you to get the flavour. See if you're interested."

Leafing through at random she came across a yellowing old letter to the *Guardian* women's page:

"Your correspondent yesterday moved me to tears. Like the writer, I too have been in love with my best friend for several years. Unlike the writer, I do not have the comfort of a husband and children. But I do not WANT to be a lesbian. My career, in government service, does not allow me that freedom. I also believe that homosexuality is morally wrong. So why is it that sometimes when I'm with her, the slightest look or accidental touch can be nearly overwhelming?"

Madeline could not read on under Shadbolt's gaze. She was amazed at the amount of background material. Enough to write a book. "Who got this stuff together?" she asked.

"Most of it was in the cuttings library, but Julie added a few bits."

There were some interesting items about Colette Bowe, the woman who planted a leak for the government over the Westland affair back in the eighties, including a sly diary piece: "The only official mole with a Royal Warrant — by Appointment to Her Majesty's Government, Purveyor of Leaks. When she shot into the public eye recently, all that the newspapers could discover was that she had a double first in economics from Oxford, and used to pose for art students at the Slade. Oxford University has no trace of her in its records, but Queen Mary College, London University, has. She was an undergraduate there and got an upper second in economics."

"Have you checked out Rosemary's educational background?" Madeline inquired.

"Roedean," Shadbolt chuckled. "We'll leave the rest to you."

"Am I right in assuming you want me to entice and entrap her?"

"Absolutely not!" Shadbolt looked hurt. "She's already sorted herself out a little friend. They're off to Greece in a couple of weeks." He smacked his lips and put his head on one side observing the effect of this revelation on Madeline.

She let out her breath. "Where do I come in?" she said.

"When we know the exact flight details, where they're staying etcetera, we'll get you a ticket. Can you use a camera?"

"I'm not a photographer . . ."

"Never mind, it's a simple job, the boys can give you a few lessons."

Madeline cut in. "Excuse me. I haven't said I'll take the job yet. I've got a few conditions." He raised his eyebrows.

"Last night I booked into Bloomsburys. I'd like to stay there for a few nights while I'm looking for something else." He nodded. "Also," Madeline went on, "I'd like the use of a Tandy and a mobile phone . . ."

"OK, OK," Shadbolt was impatient. "That's just detail." He picked up a phone: "Cash and Pay? I want you to give Miz Madeline Silver an envelope containing five grand in £50 notes. Get her signature on a receipt. It's for advance expenses authorized personally by me." He slammed the receiver down.

"Can I have two?"

"Two what?"

"Tickets, asshole!"

Sleep was impossible. The room was flooded with green light from the crackling neon sign opposite. Madeline felt as if she were in a fish tank full of electric eels. And the air conditioning was emitting icy gusts and strange engine noises. She was comforted by the presence of a small computer and mobile phone which had been delivered by courier that afternoon. They sat on a slatted wooden shelf intended for suitcases.

Her mind wandered restlessly from one thing to another. Could she find a market for her lesbian mole story? Should she engage a lawyer to force Carol to sell the house? What would become of her if she couldn't get any work? Could she consider working for Shadbolt after all? But even if she did the Rosemary assignment for him, she couldn't trust Shadbolt to give her more work. He hadn't even given her an individual contract, only the lump sum with the vague promise of more on delivery. Then in a sudden panic, she flew out of bed and tore open her briefcase. The money was still there.

Make a list, then I'll be able to sleep, she told herself. She took a notepad and pencil embossed with Bloomsburys logo. Ring Rainey she wrote, and circled it. Open new bank account. Put cash in bank. Read library cuttings. Ring Reen. Get file from Mary. She tapped her teeth nervously with the pencil. See Rosemary, she wrote jerkily. Even as she compiled the list she was conscious that she had not definitely ruled out working for Shadbolt. She had sort of assumed she would take the money then use his contacts and resources for her own story. She would have to go with the flow and see how things panned out.

When she still couldn't drift off, she took the headphones from the console next to the bed and roamed the airwaves.

Caller: "Monty . . . I don't know how you can call Greek democracy 'pure democracy . . .' "

Monty: "They were not represented by anyone — the individual was the unit of democracy . . ."

Caller: "But Monty, they had slaves!"

Monty: "Well, *they* had no say. But that's the definition of slavery, isn't it?"

Caller: "It certainly is, Monty."

Music: Dum de dum de dum. "Men! Ring now for an appointment with our expert adviser. All male problems dealt with in absolute privacy . . . just call us now and ask for the Male Care Clinic."

Madeline was soon in a deep, dreamless sleep.

chapter 14

When the wedding date was announced the press obligingly published the news, but not without raking over old ground. Soon after the press decamped, women with placards began arriving on the grassy knoll opposite. "Don't Do It, Rosie!" they yelled and passing male motorists heard them calling: "two-four-six-eight, how do you know your wife is straight!"

Mortifying! Rosemary spent most of her time in the converted attic listening to music with a pair of headphones clamped on her head, bunkered down until she and Helen could get away for their holiday. Whenever she pulled the telephone plug out of its socket, Celeste gleefully replaced it. Her enjoyment of the situation was undiminished, especially her long conversations with her new-found friend, Gresby.

"Rosie, go out and talk to those poor girls. You are their heroine!"

"Rosie, it's the TV people on the telephone, they are begging you, begging you to appear on television. Won't you do it, just once?"

"I have nothing to say."

"Read up on the subject darling, that's the only way one can improve one's understanding. One can always find something to say."

"I have never in my entire life seen you with a book, mother, except the telephone book."

"Daddy used to read all the time. He always had his nose in a book: Freud, Kraft-Ebbing, Havelock Ellis. A voracious reader, voracious!"

But the headphones were clamped tightly over Rosemary's ears and the rollicking last movement of a Beethoven piano sonata rendered her impervious to the rest of the world.

For the next few weeks, a Fortnum and Mason's van arrived regularly. They were having their meals delivered and Rosemary missed her fish and chip suppers.

The kids were at school. Terry was with Jack who had gone down with the lurgy. Fever and shortness of breath: the latest bug going round.

Jack was in a terrible state. Parrot eyes on the pillow. Motionless, rasping whine. Mary retreated. "I shouldn't be in here," she hissed. "I don't want to pass anything on to the kids. Why don't you get him cleaned up and get the doctor to him?"

"It'd cost," Terry said. "And I've got to get to work."

Because of Terry working she was not entitled to the dole. She spent hours in the dole office at Melton Street. She would never forget the sign on the wall: the benefits agency reserves the right to refuse service to anyone who is drunk. A drunk sang "I'm a graduate of the university of the SS and I can say in all consciousness that none of yous are going to get a penny . . ."

"Who's going to look after him?" Terry demanded.

"Look after who?"

"Jack."

"You're his mate," she said. And Terry packed an overnight bag and went to do his duty.

Mary could no longer look at Terry without comparing him unfavourably with Reen's son, Patrice. It was incredible that they belonged to the same species, were made of the same material. Patrice was graceful and willowy: a bewildering range of expressions animated his face when he talked. Terry's features were expressionless and his movements wooden. She now realized he was dull-witted. A paunch protruded over the top of his too-tight trousers. The sight of a v-shaped expanse of grizzled wool poking out of his unbuttoned shirt almost made her gag.

The only thing she was grateful for was that he never insisted on sex. Since the birth of the boy he had completely lost interest. A blessing she did not underestimate. The horrible sound of her father grunting and shouting as he pounded on her mother's bedroom door still haunted her as she slept. She had lain huddled on the bed with her mother, brothers and sisters. She was the baby. Their mother had barricaded herself in the room, the wardrobe and chairs stacked against the door. They rocked perilously and she heard wood splintering every time her father made one of his mad rushes at the door.

"Let me in! Let me in, Trissie!" he pleaded.

"I'm having no more children," her mother shouted. If little Mary woke in the middle of the night, she always found her mother still sitting bolt upright, ever vigilant.

"No more children! No more children!" she used to shout like a slogan, long after they had heard his footsteps retreating.

Looking back on it, Mary supposed her mother must have been about the same age she was now: only a young woman! It's depressing the way history repeats itself and no one learns a thing. Why must every generation go through the same crap again and again? If only there was an injection we could take to inoculate ourselves against the stupidities and horrors of the past.

The other day Rose had told her about her two: a boy aged fifteen and a girl of eleven. The little girl cooks and runs round after her elder brother. Rose tells her not to. "It's just like the girl imitates me and the boy imitates his dad," Rose said. The boy had complained when the girl forgot to put ketchup on a sausage sandwich she brought to him as he sat watching television.

"Why do we have to go on repeating the same crap?" When Mary asked Reen, who always had an answer, Reen said: "It only seems like that, love. If you look back how things was when your mum was young . . . you'll realize . . . things *have* moved forward."

For the first time, Mary had doubts about Reen's infallibility. "They can grind us into the dust," Reen continued, "but we'll always rise again and start from scratch, if necessary." She'd gone into one.

Madeline could have kicked Mary. Reen was getting irritable too. But Mary kept a vice-like grip on the file and turned the pages like a schoolgirl trying to prevent her neighbour from cheating.

"There's nothing in here about us," she complained. They were gathered in Reen's front room: Mary, Ruby, Reen and Madeline, who had arrived late. Herbert had found a job as a chef in an all-night grill. Rose, Mary and Ruby took turns looking after their combined kids.

"Give me that," Reen said grumpily and yanked the file out of Mary's hands. She was no better at letting the others see. But she scanned it much faster.

"It's interesting," she said at last. "Basically the whole thing's a minute book. There's a record of thanks being received for a contribution to Tory party funds but it doesn't say how much . . . then it goes on about a meeting the MD had with trade union general secretaries at the Inn on the Park . . . that's nothing new in itself. They're always knife and forking with the bosses. But they agreed to leave it up to local shop stewards to draw up competing lists for redundancy. Ah, innit nice, they've got confidence in the workers . . ."

"We know all that," Ruby said impatiently.

"True," Reen said, "but it's nice to know the details. They decided against fitting heavy eye-bolts on the ground floor doors because the unions were so co-operative. Makes you sick!" She read on silently for a while and the others waited obediently.

"Here's a gem," she read. "Due to widespread misunderstanding about Japanese penetration of British markets and real estate, it will be the duty of the paper to inform the public of the benefits of Japanese participation in our economy. The directors will shortly appoint a senior journalist as our new economic and industrial correspondent.'"

There was silence as she read on: "'Now the threat from without has receded, a survey of 'D' notices shows that subversion from within has become the main threat to society: Irish terrorism, disaffected youth, black uprisings, lesbian and gay militancy, and' . . . wait for it . . ." Reen said, "'computer crime.'"

"Boring!" Ruby said. "We're not in it."

"It covers everyone in this room, except you and me, Rubes," Reen laughed as she closed the file.

"Can I borrow it?" Madeline asked meekly, looking at Mary. Before the latter could reply Reen said, "Take it." Then she patted Mary's shoulder. "Let her plough through it, love. It'll save us the bother."

Madeline was out of her depth with the youth of today. At first she wasn't sure if he was going to acknowledge that she had spoken. He was moving his head as if listening to music.

"Yeah, Patrice is a dead cool name," she said, struggling to dredge up some groovy youth words — it was worse if you got them wrong. "I guess you were named after Lumumba?"

"Ask me mum," he said, "she's the only one who calls me it. Nobody else calls me it."

"What do your friends call you?"

"Captain Crunch."

Was he having her on? She wished she had the nerve to ask the significance of this. Then he explained. "After the first great phreaker. This geezer finds a whistle in a cornflake packet, right? He blows it down the phone, right? And you know what happens? He opens up the whole fuckin' system, man. He can call up anywhere in the fuckin' world. For free!"

"How would he know what numbers to call?"

He sucked his teeth and glanced around the walls meaningfully. Gadgets and reference books stacked up to the ceiling. Madeline was no expert but she knew a piece of hardware when she saw one. Some of the stuff was from the office.

"You got some passwords for me?" he said, sitting in front of his terminal like a maestro about to perform.

"Well, I can give you the log-on procedure and my own personal password which may get you into this system, but I only had limited access and they may have voided my password by now."

He sighed tetchily. "I'm already in the system. No sweat," he said. "And I've got Shadbolt's password, so let's go with that shall we?"

Madeline was thunderstruck. "You've got Shadbolt's password? I don't believe you! People in the office would kill for it."

"It ain't crucial. He ain't got access to the real hard-core data like finances, pension funds, payroll, and stuff like that."

"How on earth did you get it?" she said.

"My mum." He consulted a notebook dangling from a string under his desk and began key-stroking rapidly.

"She went shoulder surfing. It just means looking over an operator's shoulder," he explained. "Easy if you're dusting the desk. Makes the little cleaning job more interesting too."

"That's amazing," she said, genuinely impressed. To do it

you'd have to watch where the operator put their fingers on the keyboard. A password does not show on the screen.

"What is his password, by the way?" She tried to sound casual.

"Lou Grant," he said.

"What do you mean, Lou Grant?"

"That's it. That's the password!"

They both shrieked with laughter.

"What's your password?" he wanted to know.

"I'm not telling," Madeline said, suddenly coy.

"I'll bet I can guess it," he said.

"Never in a million years," Madeline protested.

"I'll bet you fifty quid," he persisted.

"I wouldn't take your dosh." Quickly she changed the subject. "Do you have any fax numbers?" she asked. Maybe she could contribute something useful after all. "One thing that has been done very successfully in previous disputes is feeding loo paper through the fax machines," she suggested.

"Nice!" he said absently.

"Oh shit, I've just thought, there's a problem with it."

"Hmmm?"

"It's hellishly expensive. It runs up the phone bill like there's no tomorrow."

"No worries," Patrice said. "We're hooked up to next-doors'."

Madeline did a double-take.

"Don't they notice?" she said.

"No sweat," he laughed. "They're rich, white bastards, kicked out of Azania. Thick as condensed pig shit. We're into their lecky too!"

She glowed with pleasure at being made party to all this subversion.

Exhilarated, she and Patrice worked late into the night,

planting logic bombs, inventing crazy memos for the bulletin board, sending flowers to secretaries and setting off security alerts.

Madeline had been upstairs with Patrice for hours. "What do you think they are doing?" Mary quizzed Reen.

"Buggering up tomorrow morning's paper, I hope," Reen said. Another howl of laughter came from overhead.

"You know she's . . . you know . . . one of them . . ."

"Yeah? Who says so?

"Terry," Mary replied sheepishly.

Reen grimaced. "What would he know about it?"

"Jack told him."

"Jack told him! How would he know?"

"Nell . . ."

"Sounds like a committee's been formed on the subject," Reen said disapprovingly.

"What do you think?" Mary persisted.

"I think, apart from the fact she's got her feet in the working class and her head in the bourgeoisie, she's basically okay," Reen said.

Mary shook her head in disbelief. It was shocking the way Madeline just marched in and took over. How could Reen be bluffed by such a poser? The cow had even charmed Patrice, who was usually hostile to white people and always met her admiring glances with a rude glare. Was he taken in too?

"She only wants to use us for her own ends," Mary warned. Reen was trying to proofread a leaflet.

"What are you so worked up about?" she replied, unperturbed. "She's got her agenda, we've got ours. That's life!"

Life had changed drastically for Mary. Rushing around to meetings. Plenty of energy, and she hadn't had a headache for over a week. She was learning stuff all the time. So what if her reading was slow? It was better than being so far up yourself you were coming out your own navel. Mary was proud of her quick brain and trusted her own instincts. Madeline, with all her reading and up-herself talk, was crap compared to someone like Reen. It was obvious the way she sat up and begged for that bloody file. She was like a cat on hot bricks while Mary teased her, making out she mislaid it, then finding it again, just for the fun of seeing Madeline's face. It was full of the kind of stuff everybody knows but no-one can do fuck-all about. She looked straight at Madeline as she played with the file and the silly bitch's eyes were lit up like the fourth of July. All over that one little word — "secret". Ha, bloody, ha! She kept it up till Reen started getting irritated and virtually ordered her to hand over the bloody thing. All that shit might be secret to the likes of Madeline but to people living in the real world, it's no bloody secret at all.

"Oh, Reen . . .?"

"Huh?"

"There's something I've been meaning to ask you . . ."

"Oh yeah?"

"Who are those old geezers?"

Above Reen's fireplace hung five portraits woven from grey and black silk. Unframed, they just hung there limply, attached by drawing pins.

"Marxengelsleninstalinmaozedong," Reen mumbled. Mary did not pursue it. At first she wondered if Reen belonged to some weird religious sect. But Reen always said religion was bad for your health.

chapter 15

The place was full of Americans, Germans, and their vile brats. But the coffee was good. She had only just made it in time for breakfast. Bloomsburys had its own water purifying plant. It was a long time since Madeline had taken a proper bath, immersing her whole body in hot soapy water. For months she — like other Londoners — had been using a bucket of water and a jug to wash one little bit of her body at a time, standing upright in the bathtub. Now she understood why lying in your own scummy water was considered unclean by people who traditionally used the bucket and jug method. And it wasted a lot of water.

When all the tourists had trooped off to see the sights, she dozed over the newspapers in the lounge.

"Sources close to Whitehall today expressed quiet satisfaction with the embarrassment caused to the Opposition by leaked proposals to recriminalize homosexuality. The Labour Party is squirming under pressure from gay groups and the media to state their own position on this question . . ."

Madeline knew the Opposition had been challenged by gay campaigners to get on with opposing, not just go along passively with the government's leaked proposals. But it was the same old story in the run-up to a general election, not a peep out of them, unless it was to offer support for even more racist immigration and asylum laws or dreaming up new ways of clamping down on the perennial bane of society, single parents.

When her name was paged she had worked herself up into

such a fury she didn't hear it at first.

A hand-delivered envelope awaited her at reception. It contained two tickets to Mitilini, departing in ten days.

Since she'd been staying in the hotel her shit had turned luminous yellow. It shone in the dark. She wondered if it was the eggs. Every time she washed her hands, her palms became red and itchy: similar to the sensation she used to get after a session of Tai Chi. "Look at the palms of your hands," the teacher had said, "they should be pink and mottled. It shows the chi is rising." But this wasn't anything to do with her chi.

"I've got to get out of this place," she resolved after her third night at Bloomsburys. Hotel life was expensive and the novelty had worn off.

Rainey's phone wasn't being picked up. She'd tried a million times. She didn't even know where Rainey lived, or with whom. It was surprising, when she thought about it, how little she knew about Rainey compared with how much she had blabbed about herself. It made her feel like a weak personality. No matter how many times she resolved never to do it again, it happened every time. If a woman asked her something about herself she responded compulsively, explaining herself, spilling everything out. What was wrong with her? Next morning she was always depressed, feeling like a worthless jerk. She had to redeem herself in the eyes of the woman to whom she had revealed all. Only then could she start feeling good about herself again. See? She had it all worked out. She didn't need a shrink as that bitch Carol was constantly implying.

When Rainey's sleepy voice answered, Madeline was taken aback. "Can I see you today?" she stuttered.

"What time is it?"

"Noon."

There was a pause and what sounded like a yawn. "Are you ready for Vlasta?"

"I'm getting desperate. I'm staying at Bloomsburys and it's costing me a fortune. I'm spending dough I've got earmarked for something more interesting."

Maddy could recall the days when you could go a hell of a long way on five grand.

"Shall I pick you up about four?"

"That would be marvellous," Madeline said. "I'll see you in the lobby."

After that she felt positive, light-hearted. She spent the rest of the afternoon going through her cuttings and Mary's file, making notes.

At first glance she didn't recognize Rainey. She'd never seen her out of uniform. Her hair was loose and she wore a skimpy black top and rust brown shorts with leather sandals. The effect was stunning. Madeline's palms began to itch as she crossed the lobby where Rainey sat studying an *A to Z*.

"I called Vlasta," Rainey said, skipping a greeting. "She's in. It's good timing. Catch her before she hits the bars."

A ramshackle deux chevaux, painted purple and yellow, waited in the street. It couldn't be hers! But it was. Madeline climbed into the cockpit seat and Rainey, smelling of warm cardamoms and sandalwood sat next to her. They chugged off towards south London. The weird shy feeling had returned.

"Not very talkative today?" Rainey observed.

On either side of the streets were piles of furniture and bits and pieces people had put outside their houses for sale.

Vlasta's was in a wide, leafy avenue with a driveway you could sweep in one side of and out the other. Moss-covered concrete lions guarded the steps. It was like the haunted house in a children's storybook. Madeline's hypersensitive nose picked up the peculiar odours even before the door opened, first a crack, then wide. Whoever it was opened the door, hid behind it, and did not come out till Madeline and Rainey were inside the dark hallway. Rotting fruit. Flowers. And, was it glue? A small person darted away from behind the door and disappeared. Rainey shrugged, jerked her head signalling Madeline to follow her. They went towards the sound of a piano. Rainey was screwing up her eyes as if in pain at an awful noise.

Vlasta's playing was powerful and fluid but wildly inaccurate. Somehow, to Madeline, it didn't matter. Even though it was a rambling, improvised version, she recognized one of the lesser-known Beethoven sonatas. Old theatre posters fluttered from the broken walls where, here and there, brass piping and electric wires were dangerously exposed. Bits of piano and coils of piano wire had to be stepped over. An iron frame with a cracked soundboard rested against the stairs.

They found the pianist in a huge back room, rocking backwards and forwards over a dilapidated concert grand: her head bent down between her hands as her spatulate fingers roamed the keyboard. She wore a long, black crêpe evening gown with a white rose wilting from the bodice. They stood there waiting for her to finish. Rainey muttered, "Isn't it excruciating?"

Madeline was entranced. Behind the piano, full-length windows opened out into the garden full of sunflowers and hollyhocks, giant pink and grey mushrooms, overgrown clumps of bamboo and fernery.

Abruptly, the music stopped. "I know you!" Vlasta barked. Madeline jumped. It had not occurred to her the woman would remember. She flinched under the agate-eyed stare. "I think not," she said. Vlasta growled and shook her head.

"What do you want?" she challenged Rainey. The sound of a singer practising scales floated down from the floor above. "Got any rooms vacant?" Rainey answered casually.

"I knew you'd be fuckin' after something!" Vlasta cried triumphantly. "You wouldn't be round here if you didn't fuckin' want something."

"Madeline needs somewhere to stay for a while." Rainey sounded too apologetic.

"I love your playing," Madeline interjected enthusiastically. "Maybe you could give me piano lessons?"

Vlasta curled her lip. "Do you know how long it took me to fuckin' learn to play like that? You're too fuckin' old. I started when I was three-and-a-fuckin'-half!"

A spasm which Madeline took for a smile flitted across Vlasta's lips. It encouraged her to hope. She had made up her mind she wanted to move in. The garden clinched it.

"Have you got any rooms free?" Rainey asked.

"Joe's room's vacant," Vlasta replied flatly. "I had to throw the fucker out."

"And is it an all-women house?" Madeline asked. Vlasta nodded. "It is now," she said as she hitched up her skirts and wandered out of the room without looking to see if they were following. They were. Interesting smells filled the whole house. Vlasta went from room to room opening doors for Madeline and Rainey to see. In the kitchen was a rough refectory table with six heavy wooden chairs. Copper pots and pans covered in thick dust were suspended from hooks. There was an ancient gas cooker in one corner.

It was fixed that Madeline could have a room on the first floor, overlooking the garden. Vlasta showed no interest in the transaction and Rainey talked them through it. How much is the rent? When can she collect the key? When can she move in?

"She looks Slavonic," Madeline remarked as they drove back. "Well, maybe . . ." Rainey said, "who knows? All I know is, her name's not Vlasta Balkova; it's Jean Henderson."

"How do you know?"

"Seen her passport. Born Liverpool, 1958."

"Did you know Margaret Thatcher's childhood ambition was to

be a civil servant in colonial India?" asked Celeste over tea.

"I didn't know that," Madeline said.

Celeste was a fascinating source. If only she could write it all down or use a tape recorder, but she must be discreet. She was posing as a television researcher for a programme on the British in India.

From what Celeste had told her so far, Madeline estimated that either the old lady must be getting on for a hundred years old, or was a fabulous liar. She claimed to have been present at a Claridge's ball in the twenties given by Cornelius Vanderbilt.

"Dickie met Edwina there and, almost immediately, her grandfather died leaving her millions. Millions!" Celeste stirred her tea. "A wonderful woman, Edwina. Vicious things have been written about her relationship with Nehru." She pondered, "Or was it Paul Robeson? Perhaps both."

Madeline waited, breathless at the mention of the Mountbattens.

"We were very close friends. My husband and I, Dickie and Edwina . . . she would go round the back streets of Delhi, tending sick children. Not with her bare hands, of course . . ." she trailed off looking into the distance. "We were always at Broadlands: with Maria Callas, Rex Harrison, Charlie Chaplin . . ."

"Where was your daughter at this time?"

Celeste's face clouded over. "Rosemary? Let me see, was she at school in England?"

"Did you meet any of the English writers who were living in India then?" Madeline asked, almost negligently.

"There was one. Who was that fellow? My husband didn't like him."

"Paul Scott?"

Celeste's head had fallen forward and she closed her eyes for a minute or two. When she seemed revived, Madeline resumed her interlocution.

"And you went back to India for the twenty-fifth anniversary of independence?"

"That is so," Celeste replied sadly. "We returned for the celebrations. We were treated like royalty everywhere we went."

Madeline thought of the newspaper headline: "Shots Ring Out Under Cover of Independence Celebrations". There was silence in the room and Celeste was nodding off again. Her soft tissue-paper face was still pretty. Sipping tea from fine china off a silver tray in Celeste's elegant drawing room, surrounded by artefacts plundered from India and China, Madeline forgot all about Reen and the girls.

"Human beings are living longer," Celeste croaked, "but the life expectancy of the planet is diminishing every day? What do you think of that?"

"I think we should make the most of the time we've got," Madeline began, but her philosophical reverie was shattered when an angry voice called: "Mother! Who is this?"

Flustered, Celeste put her hand behind her ear. "What did you say your name was, dear?" she asked.

"Gloria," said Madeline. "Gloria Spicer."

Next day, Rosemary had just returned from the fish and chip shop when she was again surprised to hear voices from the drawing room. Seeing Gresby sitting there so cosily, enjoying Celeste's attention and admiration, she could scarcely believe he was the same creature who'd spouted his diatribe of disgust, his lips flecked with foam. A Jekyll and Hyde character, obviously. She was on her mettle, alert for signs of a relapse. For once, feeling protective towards her mother.

In the harsh light of day Rosemary could see her first impression had been mistaken. Not only was he older than she had thought, he was much older. When she had tackled Helen about her imagined age discrepancy, Helen had laughed and said: "Well, old thing, I've only got one word to say on the subject: facelift!" The fine pleats behind his ears were clearly visible in the bright sunlight flooding the drawing room. When she caught his eye, his discomfort was palpable under her close scrutiny.

"When it comes down to it, who gives a toss whether they change the law or not?" he was saying. Celeste hung on his every word.

"Well, I do, Gresby dear," she said sweetly. "I've seen too many people's lives ruined . . ."

He seemed shocked. "When I was at prep school I was part of a queer-bashing squad and we used to write to their parents. We were actively encouraged by the school authorities."

"Well, there you are, that proves my point," Celeste said.

Gresby's revelation and his vehemence came as a complete surprise to Rosemary. More than ever, she felt a compulsion to dissociate herself from him. In her confusion she said: "Let's change the subject. Let's talk about the so-called wedding."

Celeste was delighted. "Yes, yes, yes. Get a notepad. We must make a list. What is your surname, Gresby? You're joining the family and we don't even know your name."

"Marsh. Gresby-Marsh. Hyphenated: William Gresby-Marsh. Dropped the William, it was too fussy."

Celeste bobbed up and down with excitement. "Why don't we buy the dress today! Let's go to Fenwick's! One can try on nice hats."

chapter 16

Every time she flew she was forced to think: who will care if I die? Who will care if this plane plunges into a mountain and smashes to smithereens? Flying always induced fantasies of her own death. What music will she have at her funeral? A lonely graveyard: a mysterious, cloaked figure stepping out of the shadows and placing a single rose on her coffin.

They dropped down through fluffy clouds then, suddenly, under the wingtips she saw an expanse of dazzling water.

Rosemary had forgotten how liberating it was to be away from Celeste. At the same time she thought of her mother with something like fondness now they were apart. In her luggage was a sweet little hard-covered notebook Celeste had given her in which to keep a holiday journal. This gesture touched Rosemary in a strange way. When she was a child, her father had given her a similar one in which she had written all kinds of nonsense. She burned it in the school sanitary-towel incinerator when she turned thirteen and hadn't thought of it again for thirty years. Now she wished she could read it to fill in the gaps in her memory.

As they circled her hands became damp. Oblivious to her distress, Helen sat beside her calmly turning the pages of a magazine.

If they landed safely, Rosemary swore she would start again. Make the most of her life. No more irrational fears. The worst was over. The wedding. Celeste whispering so everyone could hear. "Try not to walk like a sailor, darling." Roger not turning up as promised, Gresby supplying an angel-faced adjutant to stand in as best man. Posing for photographers on the steps of Kensington Register Office, Gresby kissing her with his lips drawn back over clenched teeth. It hurt her mouth which she kept firmly closed. To save herself from toppling she had to hook one foot around his leg in a truly ridiculous fashion and it was this pose which appeared in all the papers next morning. Celeste kept a scrapbook.

Half an hour later, they were down. Safe. Abroad. She had not been out of England since her father died. An effervescent breeze blew through the bus as they sped along a beach road to their hotel.

Their rooms were side by side. Each had her own balcony overlooking a wide, beautiful bay where catamarans raced to and fro. At night they could see the lights of tiny fishing boats returning with their catches.

Rosemary was pleased with the results of a surreptitious visit she had made to an Egyptian sugaring parlour in Hampstead. Her legs were smooth and hairless as a Fabergé egg. After the first few days she and Helen established a routine of dips in the sea before breakfast. Helen tapped softly on her door and Rosemary was always ready, wearing her swimsuit under her sundress. In spite of the imprecations of various games mistresses, she had never learned to swim and could only splash out flailing her arms, never taking her feet off the pebbly sea floor. Helen swam out strongly towards the horizon while Rosemary watched anxiously from the shore until her friend's safe return.

So far, she had to admit, being with Helen was almost as pleasant as being alone. They spent hours lazing on the beach, returning to the same spot beside a green boat every day. There was nothing much for Rosemary to write in her notebook. Just looking at it reminded her she should ring Celeste to find out how things were at home. But the thought of making the call filled her with inertia and she delayed it until one morning, as they lay reading side by side under their sun umbrellas, Helen asked: "Have you spoken to Celeste?"

"I'll do it after lunch," Rosemary replied irritably, distracted from her Barbara Pym.

At noon they picked up their things and walked across the sand in the direction of their hotel. Rosemary's feet dragged at the prospect of speaking to her mother. It was the first time Celeste had been left alone. The woman had been asked to come in five days a week instead of three, so cooking and cleaning was being taken care of. But Celeste was capable of getting into all kinds of trouble. Rosemary expected wild parties, mad-cap shopping sprees, endless telephone calls to distant places. Rosemary was always imagining that other people indulged in exotic pleasures behind her back.

"Why do we call it Greek salad, when we are *in* Greece?" Helen asked over lunch.

"I don't call it Greek salad when I'm in Greece."

"You seem out of sorts . . ."

"I'm edgy about Celeste. I sense that all is not well."

"What can she get up to . . . such an old lady?"

"You'd be surprised. She's amazingly vigorous and mentally agile."

"She seems completely gaga to me."

"She gets bored. It's nothing to do with age. She has always been the same. Boredom leads to indulgence in foolish, inappropriate behaviour," Rosemary finished.

In the deserted lobby, an English tour operator monopolized the only telephone, making wildly improbable promises to a group stranded on a remote part of the island. "Daphne will be with you soon. I've sent her off in a coach. She's on her way."

Then he called Daphne who was still in London. "Daphne, I want you on the next flight to Mitilini. I don't care what you're doing!" Rosemary got terribly wound up. "Get off that bloody phone," she bellowed.

Celeste's voice was clear and bubbly, "Why haven't you called before? We've been worried."

"Mother, is everything all right?"

"Wonderful. Everything is wonderful, darling. We're having the most fabulous time. Gorgeous food, delicious wine, delightful company . . ."

"Mother, I'm the one on holiday . . ."

"Oh, but darling, a change is as good as a . . . whatever . . . Gresby and I are treating ourselves, enjoy, enjoy . . ."

Rosemary was stunned. "Mother," she shrieked, "Mother!" Standing next to her Helen rolled her eyes: "What is this, the Bates Motel?"

Rosemary looked at her blankly. "That monster is with my mother . . . Mother, get him out of the house immediately," she shouted into the receiver. "Do you hear me, just get him out now! Out!"

The Hotel Maria was a small family-run place overlooking the same bay where the catamarans sailed up and down. The maîtresse d'hotel sat on the blue and green terrace under a vine-covered canopy, cracking nuts into a basin. As soon as she saw Madeline and Rainey get off the bus and stagger into the sun-baked road, Maria was on her feet calling: "Wanna room?"

It was amazing how readily Rainey had agreed to come to Greece. Not many people, in Madeline's experience, had the chutzpah to drop everything and go off on an unplanned trip.

"This place is idyllic," Rainey said when Maria showed them a room facing the sea. "We'll take it," Madeline said, eyeing the double bed.

Maria, dressed all in black, jingled her keys: "You teachers?" she asked.

"Yeah, teachers," Madeline said. Maria took their passports and examined them interestedly. "You no teachers," she said, "My English no so good but I see, you no teachers."

After Maria went out Rainey said, "How did you know about this place?"

"Through friends . . ."

"The same friends who got you the air tickets?"

"Er, no. That was a freebie from the travel agent who does all the bookings for the paper. It's a long story . . ." She left it vague. "This is the off season," she said. "Lesbos has got its own micro climate because of its horseshoe shape." It would have been just her luck if Rainey had turned out to be an expert on meteorology.

From the balcony Madeline could see the top of Maria's head through the vine leaves covering the terrace. A delicious smell of coffee floated up. Across the bay, built on a promontory, was a large Club-Med style hotel. When she came back into the room, she found Rainey stepping out of her shorts. "We've got our own shower," Rainey said.

"OK, you shower first. I'll sit downstairs with a book and order us an ice-cold bottle of retsina."

"What are you reading?"

"Paul Scott."

"Ugh, he was such a misogynist bastard," Rainey shuddered. "His wife ended up in Erin Pizzey's refuge and his daughter was so disturbed she committed suicide. His mind was seriously twisted. Ask yourself? An Indian man is accused of raping a white woman and that's supposed to be a metaphor for colonialism?"

"I'm only reading it for background . . . something I have in mind to write . . ."

"And what's more, the bastard caused a famine. Hundreds died."

"How?"

"Shipping rice out of India to feed British troops in Malaysia."

"I'm only reading it for research purposes . . .", but Rainey was disappearing through the door trailing her towel after her.

A donkey clopped by in front of the hotel carrying a woman sitting side-saddle and deep in thought. Madeline would like to have known what was going on inside her head. Maria called a greeting and the rider nodded. On the other side of the road there was a low sea-wall and a few yards of rocks sloped down to the water's edge. Madeline sat facing the bay. "A bottle of cold retsina, *parakalo*?" Then added, "Bring another glass if you'd like to join us."

Maria hesitated, "Your friend?"

"She'll be down soon."

Maria put the bottle and two glasses in front of Madeline. "I don't drink," she said, shaking her head, "time to cook dinner."

"Oh, too bad," Madeline said looking out across the water. "Do you know the name of that big hotel?"

"Hotel Diogenes," Maria said. "Very bad, every expensive. One day there, you can have three weeks here. Very bad food," she grimaced and drew her thumb under her throat. "Very bad pay. My son works there. A waiter. Meat in the freezer seven years," she held up seven fingers. Madeline was aghast.

"That's appalling," she said, putting down her glass. "Sure you won't have a drink?" But Maria had returned to her nuts.

Rosemary pretended not to notice Helen peeping at her from the adjacent balcony as she scribbled in her diary:

"From day one I have sensed her subtle advances and resist them assiduously. 'The water is much clearer over here' — holding out her hand. Or laughing uproariously at my feeble attempts at humour. Also, remembering small things about me which I must have let slip in an unguarded moment. Such things as one would only remember about a woman in whom one had more than a passing interest.

"I have given Celeste two days to get rid of Gresby. It is clear he is duplicitous to the core. She became abusive: 'You're no fun and you don't want anyone else to have fun. You've always been a horrible, resentful girl. Gresby's worth ten of you.' I did not dignify this with a reply. Will call her tomorrow to make sure he's gone. Nothing is going to spoil my holiday.

"Last night — a feast of bean soup, chips, omelette, Greek salad, Domestica, bread — a band struck up and a girl aged about ten danced obscenely, undulating hips, sticking her tongue and pelvis out, all dressed in pink with hair ribbons. Men leering, parents looking on proudly. This morning, breakfast in, bread rolls, tomatoes, onion and olive oil . . . siesta . . . then bought peaches, pears, peanuts, yoghurt, potato crisps, melon, ice-cream.

"Later, drank Curaçao at a bar on the beach, both had blue lips. Programme on TV about General Metaxis. Then ads, "Always" sanitary towels. Girl shown ringing date on calendar, then sitting in white ballgown with legs crossed at a rakish angle. The animals are all in good voice. A donkey makes human noises, braying You, you, you . . . Then cats screech, dogs bark and cocks crow. Cowbells tinkle and crickets sing all night.

"Saw a sick dog which made us both feel sick. She tried to drag herself along but back legs gone. A boy tried to goad her into movement. One flicked sand in her eyes and she struggled to get away from him, dragging herself further up the beach trying to find shade. For a moment reminded of London, dogs panting on pavements.

"Yesterday went with a coach load of other hotel guests. High up the mountains to a monastery. Nothing special but while there fancied I saw Lorraine Leonard!

"There was a young priest with Montgomery Clift eyes and glistening beard, white skin untouched by sun. Dainty walk. Very conscious of his prettiness; dressed up like Archbishop Makarios. Those cool marble corridors are his home and he turned a resentful glance on the intruding tourists as we paraded through the parts of the monastery which were open to the public. A chapel in the centre and the ground surrounding are barred to women. Two unruly English boys broke away from their mother and danced on the men-only ground, making faces at her. It was then I thought I saw Lorraine, walking in the other direction, some distance away."

Rosemary lifted her pen and looked across at Helen who was now arranging a wet towel and undies to dry in the sun.

"Lesbian waiters," she continued, "throw up their hands at the vast quantities of Nescafé Frappé we drink." It amused her that everyone on the island was a Lesbian. "Have you tried our Lesbian ouzo?" an old man had asked her at the beach. Not wanting to make too much of it, she didn't record this in her journal. "Tomorrow, we go to Molyvos," she wrote. Then added: "Astounded by my frequent use of 'we' in this journal — a new experience.

"We arrived in Molyvos after beautiful but perilous taxi ride. Dangerous corners marked with mini-shrines maintained by the bereaved families of those gone over the edge. Then, long exhausting climb up slanting streets full of tiny shops and restaurant bars. At a balcony which looked out over the mountainside down to the beach, had cold drinks and freshly-baked croissants. Again (and this time without doubt it was she) saw Lorraine. With a woman I've seen before but cannot place. Told Helen who was disbelieving. 'You say you're not a lesbian but we come to Lesbos and you claim to see two women you know. Really, R. I don't know what to believe.' Her mind works in a very strange way sometimes. On way back down she took picture of small girl squirming with coyness against her garden gate. Out of breath with exertion and feeling extremely irritable. I blew my top. 'It's embarrassing.' 'Why?' — 'Because she obviously hated having a camera stuck in her face.' — 'I always ask first,' Helen said, looking hurt. I was furious. She hasn't the tiniest inkling of what I've been through.

"Took snap of Helen standing in front of a sign which read 'Traditional Lesbian Pottery'."

Rainey bought books: *Women in the Greek Resistance* and *Greek Women Poets*. Madeline bought Sappho key-rings, nice presents to impress women.

The beach was packed with men lying in rows sunning their dicks and balls. "I've seen enough," Rainey said abruptly after a minute. They found a taxi to take them back to the Hotel Maria. Rainey sat in front with the driver. On the way down the mountain they stopped to pick up an English couple. The woman sat on the man's knee in the back of the car next to Madeline.

"We are from Lincolnshire," she said enunciating every syllable. "It is in northern England. How do you like it here?"

"I'm bitterly disappointed," Madeline said. "I thought Lesbos was the international mecca for lesbians but we haven't met any other lesbians at all as yet."

The woman leaned forward and tapped the driver on the shoulder. "Let us out please."

The car screeched to a halt and the couple tumbled out. Madeline and Rainey waved gaily as they drove off.

They had agreed to differ over where to eat breakfast. Rainey preferred Maria's honey yoghurt. Madeline liked the café down the road where they did bacon sarnies. "You should come with me one morning," she told Rainey. "You meet the most bizarre people."

"I'm not sure I want to meet any more bizarre people," Rainey said.

"Well, there's Mrs Holiday Tummy. She's always on about her guts. She's here with her two horrible sons. I asked if she was going on the tour to Erresos to see Sappho's acropolis . . ."

"You're the one who's bizarre," Rainey interrupted.

"Anyway . . . she said 'I'll have to have a few words with my husband. He's very good. He lets me do what I like.' Then she asked him and he said 'You don't want to go on your own.' So she's not going. Sometimes you forget how lucky you are to be a dyke."

Their pattern was: rise between 8.30 and 9.30, go for breakfast, lie on the beach, read and swim between trips to the bar for fruit juice and beer; siesta between six and nine in the evenings, then out to eat in a taverna.

"The sky is so beautiful it could make you cry to leave it," Rainey said. The lights of mountain villages twinkled in the dark. The red and green sodium lights of small fishing boats bobbed across the water. The chugging sound of their engines only became discernible as they came alongside the pier. Most nights Madeline and Rainey ate at the same place. They called it the Blue Lagoon because the interior was painted different shades of sea blues and greens. But no-one sat inside. The patrons sat at tables near the boats. Wild dogs and cats hovered round the tables waiting for scraps of food. One night Madeline got a little tipsy and fought off a large dog, using a chair and looking like a lion tamer in a circus act.

They ate garlic dip made with potatoes, little pastry rolls with a trace of ham in them, fried aubergines, cooked *pekora*-style with cheese, feta salad and chips.

When Madeline sent a few reverse-charge faxes to Patrice,

boosting the South African neighbours' phone bill, Rainey's reaction was way OTT. "We're on holiday. Can't you leave the bloody fax machine alone?"

Then when she came back from a swim before breakfast one morning, Madeline found Rainey sprawled on the bed with all the Rosemary files spread round her.

"What the fuck have you brought this lot on holiday for?"

"How dare you go through my stuff?"

"I want to know what we're doing here. Why all the electronic gadgetary and zoom lenses?"

Suddenly Madeline felt stupid. It was a mistake to have asked Rainey to come to Greece. Showing off. And now her half-baked plan to spy on Rosemary for Shadbolt was going to be found out by the very person whose respect she wanted to win. She didn't know what to say.

"You've got no right to go through my stuff," she repeated.

"Is Rosemary here?" Rainey demanded. "Is that what you're up to?"

"I'm going for a shower," Madeline said stomping out of the room, leaving wet feetmarks behind her. The whole adventure was ruined because she had failed to think things through properly. She took as long as possible showering, hoping Rainey would go away and leave her alone.

She did not. Rainey was still reading.

"It's all quite fascinating," she said, as Madeline entered the room. "All this material you've collected about the father. 'The crème de la crème of the closet classes — closet cases in high places' — how's that for a headline?" Madeline didn't respond.

"What exactly do you intend to do with all this information?"

"I just felt there was a story in it somewhere," Madeline said. "And, as you know, I am a journalist."

"Why don't you get an honest job?" Rainey said.

"What? Like ferrying leaders of the capitalist patriarchy about in Rolls Royces?"

Rainey laughed. "Don't talk crap."

"As a matter of fact, you're right. I was asked to do a job on Rosemary. That's how I got the tickets. But I've got no intention of spying on her. I wanted to write something about the way in which she was set up. See, I was in the office the night the story was planted in the paper. I know exactly how it was done and who did it."

"So, why not talk to her and try doing something with her co-operation and approval instead of all this zoom lens crap?"

"How?"

When Rosemary and Helen arrived back at their hotel there was an urgent message waiting for Rosemary. RING HOME. She looked at her watch. Seven pm local time, 9 pm GMT. The "home" suddenly struck her as preposterous. "Home" was hardly an accurate description of the household she shared with Celeste. The only part of the house she might call home was the attic music room. She asked the receptionist to get the number and when she turned around, Helen had disappeared without even saying "see you at dinner". Rosemary went to her room to wait for her call to Celeste.

She kicked off her sandals and stretched out on the bed. Her head ached. Right at this moment, she realized, she was too upset about Helen going off to worry about whatever it was Celeste had to say. The ring of the telephone made her jump, even though she was expecting it.

"He's gone," Celeste wailed. "It was terrible. Yesterday a nasty man smoking smelly cigars burst into the house with a posse of photographers. They were taunting poor Gresby, saying you've gone on honeymoon with your girlfriend! He said he couldn't take any more. After that he left. And he hasn't been back. I'm so worried. You don't know to what extremes a sensitive man like Gresby can be driven. You must come back at once!"

"Mother, don't worry. Now Gresby's gone you've got nothing to worry about. I'll come back soon, calm down now."

"You don't understand. It's Gresby I'm worried about. He was terribly shaken. Not in a fit state to be alone. I want to look after him."

"Mother, cut it out. I'll ring you in the morning when I've had time to think."

Drained, she replaced the receiver and buried her head in the pillow. It was morning when her eyes snapped open. Nine o'clock and Helen had not come to her door. A dry sobbing noise began. At first she could not work out where it was coming from. Or why? Catching her breath, she dragged herself from the bed, slowly undressed and went to the bathroom. Twice as she stood under the fine jet of water she thought she heard a knock at the door and leapt dripping out of the shower. She draped a towel around herself and stood by the door calling "Helen?" but there was no answer.

chapter 17

Mary was having the time of her life. They met regularly at Reen's. When they watched telly for news about their campaign she saw herself and the others shouting and waving placards outside the newspaper office.

"Patrice and Madeline have done a fantastic job," Reen said as another old geezer came on to complain about the serious blow to press freedom. "Bloody fantastic." Reen had just given up smoking again and gave out bad vibes every time Mary lit up.

"She's buggered off," Mary said resentfully. "And I'm not saying that just because she's, you know . . . a dyke."

"Why don't you stow it then, Mary? Aren't you the one always going on about making the same mistakes over and over? Why don't you learn something for a change? Do something about your attitude."

Mary was livid.

Another item came on about hacking and jamming.

"Papers have come off the presses containing phoney stories and mangled sentences," the newsreader reported. The group around Reen's telly whistled and cheered. "Spot the diff," Reen said when the row had died down.

The newsreader looked out sternly: "The Government have said very severe penalties will be imposed on the culprits when they are caught. Systems analysts are baffled by self-perpetuating logic bombs. Counter-moves to deal with worms in the software immediately set off a whole chain of fresh problems."

Amid the laughter, Mary suddenly asked: "Could Patrice go to jail?"

No-one answered. She remembered all the equipment they'd smuggled out before the lockout. Maybe they'd all end up inside. The thought of it didn't bother her. So, Terry would have to look after the kids. He'd probably dump them on his mum.

Now Shadbolt was shown emerging from the building. A microphone was stuck in front of his face. "These people are losers," he said, waving his arm towards the pickets. "A bunch of cleaners and cooks can't intimidate us. We will not compromise press freedom."

"Bastard! Arrogant poultice!" Mary was weak with rage. "I'd like to wrap them armbands of his round his balls and string him up from the chandelier at work." That made them all laugh.

Afterwards, they decided to set up a roster for picking up Mary and Rose's kids from school. They brought them to Reen's where they could play in the garden. Patrice agreed to keep an eye on them from his window. Herbert did all the cooking and there was always a big pot of food on the stove. People came to eat or just crash out. Going home was a drag. The kids loved it at Reen's. It was a healthier atmosphere than being stuck in a poky flat. Kids need stimulation or they grow up dull. Mary was getting hers now. Better late than never.

Rosemary lifts her feet off the bottom and begins floating on her back. She creates a gap. Three seconds in which her mind is empty, fear suspended. In that gap she doesn't care about anything. She lets go completely and her legs rise. She is floating, spread out in a star shape looking at the sky. The secret is *not caring*. Flip over and start swimming.

In the cramped reception area at Snow Hill nick, Mary and Ruby sat knee to knee, waiting for their statements to be taken.

Mary's cop was tall, pin-headed and ridiculously courteous. Ruby's was older and hard-bitten, more Mary's idea of how a cop should look. One of the PCs who attended the pickets passed through the room with a mug of tea in his hand. Mary covered the lower half of her face with a magazine. His eyes panned the room without a flicker of recognition. Not that it mattered. They were not making any secret of where they were going. Like any other concerned citizens, they had come in voluntarily to report something suspicious.

They were taken to different interview rooms. Nothing to worry about. Well, they had gone over their statements dozens of times. A friend, Herbert (we don't know his other name), dropped us at Waterloo. We were walking (proceeding by foot) from the south side of the river, up the steps by the Dog and Duckett, onto Blackfriars Bridge. We heard noises like a scuffle then saw a man run across the bridge to a car. He drove off northwards. We looked over the bridge and saw a man in the water. Did you see the man being pushed? No. Did you see any physical contact whatever between the two men? No. Did you recognize either of the men? No. Did you hear a splash? No. Was the man in the water clothed? Yes. Could you make out what he was wearing? A striped shirt. Nothing else? Couldn't be sure. Did you see the man who drove off throw anything in the river that could have been clothing? Nothing. We only saw him running, getting in the car, driving off.

There were three desks in the room and three sets of interviews being carried on simultaneously. It was difficult to concentrate. There had been a serious coach crash. A young man said he had been driving down a slip road and may have caused the crash by coming out in front of the coach. A girl, his sister, was a passenger. A policeman finished taking the boy's statement then turned his attention to the girl. "Since you're under sixteen we can't interview you without your parent or guardian present. It seems a shame to bring your mum all the way down here doesn't it? It is all right for you to be interviewed by an officer of the same sex, if you consent. Would you consent to being interviewed by a WPC?"

The girl nodded.

"OK I'll go and get one."

Mary's gangly copper was busy finding a pen and left the room several times before they could get started, once for the pen and again for the correct forms for taking statements. Mary tried to read the folder he had left open on the desk.

The cop who had gone for a WPC returned. "Who did you get? Debbie?" another cop asked expectantly.

"No, Ingrid." They groaned.

The tall pin-head came back with the forms.

"Would you like to write this yourself or shall I write it as you tell me?"

"If you've got a set form, why don't I tell it and you write it, then you can prompt me by asking questions?"

He seemed pleased. "That's the way it's usually done."

First he went over the facts. "Date: Sunday 27 October, agreed?"

"I know it's Sunday, but I don't know the date."

He showed her his watch. "Just to make sure you're happy with that. OK?"

"Sure. I'm happy."

Then the time. That was easy. "Herbert dropped us at 2 am and we'd been walking for about twenty minutes."

"Two-twenty am? Happy with that?" His handwriting was cramped like a child's and he kept making errors and crossing them out.

"You'll have to initial all these alterations, I'm afraid."

When she read it through before signing, she had to stifle a laugh. He had changed everything into police jargon. Where she had said "I've never seen them before," he had written "I have no previous knowledge of the two men."

The whole tortuous process took nearly three hours. Ruby was still not out from her interview. Mary settled down to wait in reception.

They climb up to Blackfriars Bridge and are just about to step onto it when they both stop. "What's that?" Neither of them moves a muscle. Mary can hear the Thames rushing against the stanchions under the bridge. Now the drumming of feet. They both crane their necks to see. A man flings himself into a car and roars off. "YBS . . . quick, write it down," Ruby orders. "I'll remember it," Mary says. A second man is lurching towards them. She sees his bulging eyes and bloodied face. "Well, what a nice surprise," she says. "Fancy us losers meeting you here, Mister Shadbolt." As he reaches them he stumbles.

"Sla . . . a . . . gs . . ." they hear him gasp as he bumps down the steps.

"Well, that's charming."

"Very charming."

"What did you say you'd like to do to him?" Ruby asks.

Gingerly they go down the steps and bend over the man on the ground. "I'd do it if I had me rubber gloves," Mary whispers. "I'm not touching the dirty fecker with me bare hands."

"Here," Ruby offers a clean tissue and watches as Mary gets on with it. "You seem to know what you're doing girl," she says admiringly.

"Worked in a prostate ward back home, didn't I?"

"Wakey, wakey!" Ruby stood in front of her.

"Finished?"

"Yes, about bloody time."

Neither of them said anything more till they were out in the muggy night air. "How was it for you?" Mary asked.

"We done the right thing, girl. Did you see that patrol car prowling round after?"

"After what?"

"After . . . you know, after what you done . . ."

"*We* done!"

"Whatever . . . I'm telling you, we done the right thing coming forward. We can rest easy now. It might be days before they find it. And when they do, blondie in the white car is gonna have a lot of explaining to do."

Madeline is sitting in Andy's English café eating egg on toast when in comes Mrs Holiday Tummy, brandishing a newspaper.

"Whatever will they get up to next?"

"Who?"

She looks all round. "Men," she whispers.

The coffee curdles in Madeline's stomach as she reads the headline: "Shot His Bolt: Editor in Kinky Sex Drowning. Controversial editor Colin Shadbolt was fished out of the Thames last night. Police suspect an auto-erotic fatality".

Madeline visualizes a bloated Shadbolt floating on top of the water, seen from underneath like William Holden in *Sunset Boulevard*.

"What does it mean?" asks Mrs Holiday Tummy. "An auto-erotic fatality?"

"Maybe it happened like this. He was driving along, having a wank, forgot to look where he was going, and ended up in the river," Madeline says.

"Yes. That's what I thought. I thought the same."

The story is uninformative. Only one fact is clear: Shadbolt is dead. She has to get back to Maria's and get on the fax to Patrice for more news.

Rosemary strides up the beach and there, under the sun

umbrella with the usual pile of English newspapers, is Helen.

"Where have you been?"

"I thought we could do with some time away from each other."

"How did you come to that conclusion?"

"One doesn't have to be an Einstein."

Rosemary is stymied. She changes tack.

"It was incredible, Helen, did you see? I've learned to float. I swam a few strokes."

"I saw," Helen replies coldly.

"I made a fantastic discovery out there," Rosemary confides, "if letting oneself go doesn't come naturally, one can do it as an intellectual exercise. It is a mental breakthrough."

"Hmm . . ."

Experimentally, Rosemary runs her gaze over Helen's glistening body, testing her proclivities. She does not feel moved in any way.

"Don't drip all over me," Helen complains.

Rosemary picks up her towel. "I've decided to become a lesbian," she says, watching Helen's face. Her friend does not bat an eyelid. "Well, bully for you, old thing. I hope you'll be very happy."

"The problem is," Rosemary continues, rubbing herself vigorously, "I don't know the protocol."

"What on earth do you mean, protocol?"

"Well, how do I go about becoming one? Should I announce it to the press?"

"Wasn't it the press who announced it to you, dear?" Helen asks with asperity. "As far as I can see, you were the last person to know."

"Yes, but that was before I decided for myself to become one."

"What difference does it make?"

"It will make a tremendous difference to me! I will not have to keep up the pretence of being married to that wretched Gresby. I can be a lesbian and remain celibate if I wish. It will mean a different lifestyle, meeting interesting women, having friends with similar interests . . ."

"Well, it's a free country, so they say . . . but before you get carried away, old girl, I want to ask if you've seen the papers?"

"No."

"Have you spoken to your mother recently?"

"Not for a couple of days. Gresby has gone so there is nothing to worry about."

"Don't be so sure," Helen says, spreading out a newspaper. "You had better cast your peepers over this."

Rosemary reads, uncomprehending, trumped again by Helen. Her new-found confidence is dwindling by the second. She suspects Helen of *schadenfreude*. There she sits, waiting like a sage to explain life, human behaviour, popular culture, and protocol, to poor, idiotic Rosemary.

"I have heard of auto-da-fé, of course," she says slowly. "But what is an auto-erotic fatality?"

Helen bites her lip. "As far as I know, from the little I have read, it entails strangling oneself while simultaneously masturbating. God only knows how. They must be contortionists."

"Do women do it?"

"Never heard of it. However there is no accounting for taste. But who cares about that? For God's sake Rosemary, didn't you see the piece about the police looking for a blond man driving a small, white car, registration number YBS? That is what I was drawing to your attention, not that unspeakable man's watery end. Doesn't your number plate begin with the letters YBS? Isn't your car small and white?"

Rosemary snorts. "Small white man driving blond car?"

Helen rises up on her pointy elbows. "For crying out loud

Rosemary, you've picked a damn fine time to develop a sense of humour. This is terribly serious. All this publicity! Roger is going to be ropeable. The poor old queen only married me to avoid drawing attention to himself. Imagine how *he* must be feeling. Don't you get it? Anyone associated with you and Gresby is going to look ridiculous, even the straight chaps will be suspect now. It really is the limit! You and I will have to part company. I'm going to stay on here till things cool down. You go back and face the music on your own. I'm very sorry old girl, but that's the way it has to be. It's a funny old world. And, please, whatever you do, keep my name out of it!"

Rosemary is in her room packing. She cannot help giggling about the silly conversation she has just had with Helen. A few days ago she was crying over the woman, and now the spell is broken. Since her early teens, there was always some woman or other. A teacher, a woman on a train, her driver. Remote, unattainable. Now she has become the woman everyone else apparently took her for in the first place, and, hey presto, her fantasizing abruptly ends.

As she zips up her Vuitton bag, the telephone rings. A woman's voice gabbles.

"Please don't hang up on me. I know you were framed. I can help you. I'm a journalist. I used to work on Shadbolt's paper."

"Slow down," Rosemary says. "I'm listening."

"I believe it would be in your best interests to talk to me rather than the hacks waiting to pounce on you at Heathrow. We can fly to Leeds or Manchester. I've got contacts there. I promise, no harassment. We'll film the interview up there. You'll have full control over the contents. What do you say? Will you let me help you?"

Madeline and Rainey were in bed with a sheet pulled up over

their heads. Suddenly the fax began chattering excitedly, spewing out details of Shadbolt's death.

"Can't you turn that bloody thing off?"

"No. I asked Patrice to send me everything he can get his hands on."

"How romantic! Lying here in a state of post-orgasmic bliss, then that bloody thing starts up like a fart in a bottle."

"Sorry . . ."

The machine stopped. Madeline was dying to get up and read what Patrice had sent. Rainey snuggled closer. "When you asked me to come to Greece it was only the second time we had met."

"Third."

"I was bowled over."

If Madeline stretched out her arm she could almost reach the papers in the fax tray.

"Oh, for God's sake Madeline, you're just not with me, are you? You're fucking absent!" Rainey sat up and hung her legs over the side of the bed.

"I'm sorry," Madeline said, "It's just that I've got to start thinking about getting ready to go to the airport."

"What time's your flight?"

"Four. We're flying to Athens first, then getting a connection to Leeds."

"Why Leeds?"

"Some women I know have got a little film company . . . after that I might take Rosemary to Vlasta's. She'll need to lie low for a while."

Rainey lay back on the bed and stretched her arms over her head. "It won't be the same here without you," she yawned, "p'raps I'll go to another island."

chapter 18

Mary was stuffing sheets into the washing machine when the phone warbled. All she could hear when she picked it up was loud crackling. Then a little, tinny voice.

"It's me, Nell. Is that you Mary? Can you hear me?"

Mary shook the phone and shouted, "I hear you." Her own words bounced back in her ears.

"Don't say anything. Just listen. I'm in trouble. Jack won't help. It's down to you. You've got to help me. I can't talk long. I'm under arrest. Some argy bargy about papers not in order. These people can't understand one word of English. I'm in a detention centre. They've taken all my money. Can you hear me? I'm being held prisoner. Ring the Home Office. I'm a British subject. They've got to get me out."

"Where are you?"

"Koala Jumper. Somewhere half-way between India and Japan. They're all darkies here."

"What!"

"You've got to help me. Do something!"

"You must be joking, racist bitch! I hope they throw the key away!"

Terry had crept in and was lurking in the doorway as she smashed the phone down. "Who was you screechin' at?"

"Just a nutter. A nutter who deserves to be locked up."

"Where are the kids?"

"With a friend."

He didn't ask what she was doing, where she was going, or anything about her run-in with the police. "What's me and Jack gonna do when we run out o' them frozen dinners?"

"Search me."

Party time! At first Mary tried to get out of it. Reen accused her of being too chicken to go to one of them dykey parties. It was true. What would happen if one of them jumped on her? Tried it on with her? She shivered. But she couldn't even use the excuse of the kids. Reen had fixed up for Herbert and Patrice to mind them. Everyone was going. She had to go.

When she got there, a weirdo in a bunny suit with floppy ears answered the door then scuttled upstairs. Jesus, the place was falling down. It looked posh from the outside, with all the ivy and lions, but inside was tatsville. If you touched one of them loose wires hanging out of the walls you'd fry. And it stank of glue and . . . rotting fruit? Someone was thumping a piano. She followed the sound. At the back of the house she found a room the size of the place they held their union meetings. A woman with rats' tails hair, wearing a black evening dress, was playing "In My Sweet Little Alice Blue Gown" and a thin scratchy voice was singing. It came from the oldest person Mary had ever seen, an old crone all tarted up in mauve feathers.

At first she couldn't see any of her mates. Had she come to the wrong house? It was a relief when she recognized Reen's familiar head poking over the back of an easy chair. She was smoking a spliff. Then, through the long windows overlooking the back garden, she spotted Rose and Cynthia examining plants. She sat down on the arm of Reen's chair watching the performance. Mary was wearing her girliest dress so there could be no mistake.

"Where is everyone?" she asked.

"Madeline's gone to the airport to pick up her girlfriend and

Rosemary hasn't come down yet. We're early."

"What time's the programme?"

"Not until ten but she did say to arrive between eight and nine."

"Where's the booze?"

"In the kitchen. But I want a word with you, my girl, before you go getting legless." Mary felt Reen's fingers digging into her forearm.

"Ruby's told me the lot. It was crazy, doing what you done. What got into you?"

"I was angry."

"So you wraps his armbands round his balls and chucks him in the river?"

"Seemed like a good idea . . ."

"Leave it out! What if you'd been seen?"

"We wasn't. Where's Rubes?"

"She's gone after a job."

"What bloody job?"

"Bingo caller in Camden."

"Well, that's nice, that's bloody nice." If Ruby got another job, it wouldn't be the same. The music stopped. Reen and Mary applauded politely. The old crone tottered over and fell onto a nearby couch.

"Oh my, singing takes it out of one. Would someone be kind enough to bring me a scotchy wotchy?"

Mary and Reen looked at each other. Reen's hair had been fluffed up and she was wearing eyeliner.

"What are you looking at? If you're thinking I look peculiar, it's Patrice's fault. He's always trying to get me to smarten meself up."

"I thought Ruby would have stuck by us."

"She will, she will. Herbert's got another job and he still gives us a helluva lot of support."

"Oh, I hate parties," Mary protested bitterly. Then the pianist called out:

"Well, what are you waiting for, Christmas? Get the poor old bugger a drink!"

"I'll go," Reen said, getting up. Mary went over to the couch.

"You may call me Celeste. Are you another of Rosie's friends? I didn't know she knew so many lovely girls. Only Helen. But now it transpires she had all of these interesting friends. Such a secretive girl."

"Ah, well, I'm a friend of a friend . . ." A bit of a lie, but Madeline *had* invited her . . .

"My dear, did you know my lovely son-in-law has been falsely arrested and my daughter's car is in police custody."

"Heavy."

"I tried to tell them he might do something foolish . . ." she sighed. Mary saw the old woman's head slump forward. She hoped she was only having a snooze.

Just then, her attention was attracted by the arrival of a posse of young, shiny females, all wearing smart outfits, some in flash tuxedoes with tails and pointed shoes, others in flouncy dresses and high heels.

"Vlasta! Vlasta! Haven't seen you in yonks. Kissy kissy," they said in unison.

Behind them, Madeline swanned in with her "friend" who didn't even look like one. Surprisingly glam. Gorgeous even, Mary had to admit. Trust bloody Madeline to find someone like that. And only Madeline was so far up herself she'd invite everyone to come and watch her on telly!

Coyly, Rose and Cynthia tiptoed in through the french windows. Vlasta immediately jumped up and pushed them forward to be introduced, patted and hugged. At the same time, Reen returned with a bottle of Rémy Martin, too late for Celeste who was gently snoring with her little birdy mouth wide open. Mary watched in horror as Madeline grabbed Reen and smooched her on both cheeks. And Reen went pink and looked as if she was well into it. Mary averted her eyes. She shouldn't have come. She was wearing the wrong clothes. Naff. Reen was pissed off with her, and everyone else was ignoring her.

Cynthia and Rose both wore their hair swept up with sparkly tops and spangly earrings. Done up to the nines. Rose was holding Cynthia's little finger.

Every minute more and more women streamed in through the door. Music stands were set up by the piano and three women began playing trombone, trumpet and drums. Vlasta joined in on the piano. Nice jazzy rumbas. Mary had always wanted to learn the drums. She loved Latin music. She could scarcely keep her feet still. A couple of women were dancing expertly as if they'd been practising together, switching their buns in the proper Latin way. Although she was shocked to see Cynthia and Rose making fools of themselves, twirling, cheek to cheek, she felt better after a couple of stiff drinks. As she got up to do a little dance on her own, Reen sashayed past with a woman who had a posh fog horn voice and dead white hair.

"Are you the Mary who hates parties?" called Reen.

Mary giggled and wondered if it would be all right to cut in.

Madeline was nervous before the party. But everything was going swimmingly. "Do you know you're the sexiest woman in the room?" Rainey asked her. "Second sexiest," Madeline breathed back.

"Guess what," Rainey whispered. "While I was upstairs getting into my glad rags, I heard Vlasta offering Rosemary piano lessons."

"Well, fuck me!"

"I will later . . ."

"What's she got that I haven't got?"

"A Roedean accent, darling. Like a lot of working-class heroines, Vlasta is a sucker for an upper-class accent."

Madeline felt vaguely uncomfortable. "Did you know Rosemary coughed up for the booze?"

"Good for her. Who made the canapés?"

"Vlasta. With her own fair hands. She says they're a Ukrainian speciality. If you believe that, you'll believe anything."

Vlasta was a hyperactive hostess. One minute she was knocking out a number on the piano, next she was running upstairs, only to disappear for ten minutes before suddenly reappearing with more food.

Esme Evans took charge of arrangements for watching the programme. At 9.30 she wheeled in a TV set and started moving chairs into a semi-circle around it. "Where's Rosemary?" everyone was asking.

Upstairs, Rosemary lay soaking in a tub. Vlasta had made countless trips carrying pans of boiling water, adding aromatic oils to the bath and lighting candles. No-one had ever spoiled Rosemary in this way before. (Vlasta could play the piano too.) It was a ritual cleansing. Washing away the old life before commencing the new.

The interview had been a revelation, a distinct pleasure, as she imagined it must be to have a lovely job one enjoyed. Over several days they spent hours formulating questions which Rosemary was comfortable with. Nothing sensational. Plenty of time for unhurried, well-thought-out responses. Extracts from news reports preceded the interview itself. Madeline had recorded a voice-over explaining her own role. How she suspected from the beginning that Rosemary was an ingenuous pawn. How Rosemary's life had been disrupted, her hounding by the press, her terrible isolation, now over. Rosemary was amazed by her own image on the screen, how confident she appeared and sounded. They were both wearing new outfits which they had bought especially to wear in front of the cameras. Rosemary had asked Madeline to help her choose. "I'm no style guru," Madeline said modestly.

"Oh yes you are," Rosemary responded.

The pleasant sound of women laughing gaily, mingled with dance music, drifted up. She wondered what Helen was doing? Whether she would see the programme? How would she react if she could see Rosemary now? She can stay in the closet for all I care, Rosemary thought.

For the first time since his death, she was able to think composedly about her father. Everything she had been told about his assassination she had taken at face value, until now. Now she was questioning everything, including her father's death. As Madeline had pointed out: no-one had been arrested for the crime, no murder weapon had ever been found. Was suicide a more likely explanation of his death? Rosemary pictured him standing to attention, saw his ramrod spine bristle as he held his pistol to his temple.

When confronted with this theory, Celeste became distraught in her usual melodramatic fashion.

"Let the dead bury their dead. Let them rest in peace!" She wailed.

"But mother, I need to know for my own peace of mind."

"After I've passed over to the other side, you will know as much as I know, you won't have to wait long."

"Just tell me, is there any connection between his death and my case?"

"I will say no more on the subject. Please don't badger me."

"Do you know why Sir Gregory selected me to use as his scapegoat?"

"Darling, how many women are there in the department who

walk like Tugboat Annie? You have steadfastly refused to wear pretty dresses."

Vlasta was on hand to drape a towel around Rosemary as she stepped out of the bathtub. Her long legs were still smooth and hairless. Vlasta helped her dry herself. With her gappy teeth, yellow fingers and lank hair, Vlasta was like a friendly witch in the eerie candlelight.

"Do you think I walk like a sailor, Vlasta?"

Vlasta laughed like a drain.

Descending the rough wooden stairs, Rosemary noticed all eyes turn towards her. Women clapped their hands and made whooping noises. Some sat in chairs near a television set and others danced to a three-piece band. She waved, trembling with excitement. How would she cope with watching herself in front of a roomful of strangers? Was the programme as good as she thought it was?

Madeline brought a woman over to meet her. "This is Esme Evans."

"I was at school with you," said Esme. "You were a couple of years junior to me, I believe."

Rosemary had seen those brilliant blue eyes before.

Ten minutes before ten, the music stopped. Esme picked up a whisk and splashed the cymbals on the drum kit to get attention.

"Only a few minutes before the programme, ladies, so would you all please top up your drinks and take your seats."

Madeline tasted the excitement and relished the acknowledgement. She saw Rainey renewing her acquaintance with Rosemary. They were chatting over a drink. Reen and the girls looked as though they were having fun. Even that sour bitch, Mary.

Five minutes to go and a commotion broke out near the door.

People pushing into the room. Men in suits. And, with them, Carol! They burst into the room, flinging papers all over the place.

"This is a private party," Esme boomed flapping her arms as if to shoo the intruders away.

"Nothing is private in the eyes of Jesus," shouted Carol. "He can see into every nook and cranny."

"Get the fuck out of here," screamed Madeline in anguish. "You're ruining my evening."

Mary plucked one of the flying leaflets from the air. "Sexual Redemption Society . . ." she read.

"Join us sisters," Carol implored. "Save yourselves in Jesus. Leave this devil's workshop and join us. Praise the Lord!"

On hearing these words, Mary was galvanized into action. She rushed at Carol. "How dare you tell us how to live our lives, you Bible-banging hypocrites!" She drew back her fist, preparing to bash Carol. Reen grabbed her from behind.

"Cool it now, love," Reen cajoled her and led her back to her seat.

"Well done," Cynthia and Rose clucked and patted. "Well done. You told 'em."

As they watched, Rosemary drew herself up to her full, magisterial height.

"If you don't fuck off out of here, I'll set the dawgs on you," she said. Women began ululating and chanting, "Out, out, out!" and Mary and the others joined in. The three gatecrashers retreated, chased by Vlasta wielding a flue-brush.

Ghostly music issued from the television set. "Quickly, quickly, into your seats, it's starting."

Madeline's face appeared on the screen and the linkwoman announced: "In just a moment, Madeline Silver interviews the woman at the centre of the controversy surrounding the government's plans to recriminalize homosexuality . . ."

Celeste jerked awake as if a puppeteer had tugged her strings. "Look, it's Gloria!" she cried pointing to the screen.

"Shut up mother!"

". . . after the break, in an exclusive interview on this channel only . . ." announced the television set. "We present *The Lesbian Civil Servant.*"

Founded in 1986, Serpent's Tail publishes the innovative and the challenging.

If you would like to receive a catalogue of our current publications please write to:

FREEPOST
Serpent's Tail
4 Blackstock Mews
LONDON N4 2BR

(No stamp necessary if your letter is posted in the United Kingdom.)

Absence Makes the Heart
Lynne Tillman

'In *Absence Makes the Heart* Lynne Tillman lures us onto unfamiliar ground with utterly persuasive, utterly duplicitous candor. Once there, we shall never be brought safely home. Her writing leaves our assumptions about life and art a shambles and, because it is funny and revealing, we relish it; but, reader, beware — you will be getting more than you either expect or deserve.'   HARRY MATHEWS

'Lynne Tillman has the strongest, smartest, most subtly distinct writer's voice of my generation. I admire her breadth of observation, her syntax, her wit.'   GARY INDIANA

'These bizarre short stories make alluring reading.'
Time Out

Ocean Avenue
Margaret Wilkinson

"In her first novel, Wilkinson confidently and evocatively blends the historical and personal . . . into a disturbing yet funny tale." *Publishers Weekly*

"Wilkinson's original, witty, insightful novel has a surreal quality. Her characters are sad, hilarious, wonderful." *Jewish Chronicle*

"An impressive debut." *She*

"Through it all there glows a sense of place, of history and identity combined with a wistful wryness." *Sunday Times*

"*Ocean Avenue* is like a photograph album, each chapter a cameo portrait of a member of the family, an event in the family history, each staking its claim to attention. 'It was talking with authority about the human heart that intrigued me. Like novels,' says the narrator. *Ocean Avenue* is both authoritative and tentative in its approach to the heart: serious in intent, self-deprecatingly, affectionately funny in the telling." GILLIAN ALLNUTT

Transmission
Atima Srivastava

"The plot of *Transmission* is perfectly formed, and the characters strong . . . a fast, complicated book."
The Independent

"A compulsive look at straight, young non-drug users with HIV, inter-racial relationships and the ethics of working in TV . . . A socially-conscious London novel that refuses to take itself too seriously." *The Face*

"Comedy that is both bleak and tender, sharp-edged portraits of media makers and monsters, a wry look at urban styles of love and survival by a born story-teller." MICHÈLE ROBERTS

"*Transmission* is a new novel that has everything: sex, glamour, politics, friendship, excitement, and a conscience." *Northern Star*

"The writing is sharp and punchy . . . while the engaging descriptions of Angie's cross-cultural family life provide a wealth of insights into British ethnic experience. The novel's major strength, though, is in steering clear of either sermonising or trivialising while exploring difficult and challenging subjects." *Scotland on Sunday*

"This is the first great novel of 1992!"
Events South West

Alex Wants to Call It Love
Silvia Sanza

"The characters alternately search for connection and long for solitude; Sanza is adept at conveying the frustrations of failed intimacy and the rarity of true communication between even the closest of friends."
Publishers Weekly

"Sanza's debut is cute and observant in targeting the vacuity of urban life." *The Independent on Sunday*

"Crushes unwanted characters like cockroaches, but it still manages to reclaim Lower Manhattan for the human race. It bounces on a rich diet of gall and schmaltz, cheerfully cushioned by 'the humour of getting by.' The low-life scrapes mask high-minded aims. Large ideas – about chaos and the art that tames it – sneak up through the wisecracks."
The Observer

"*Slaves of New York*, Sanza style." *Elle*

"Explores death, love, work, writing and why people do all these things. Silvia Sanza writes from an original and exciting angle that keeps you surprised and, ultimately, satisfied." KATE PULLINGER

"Alex may want to call it love but Silvia Sanza is more likely to diagnose lustful anomie. With her bleak precision and Martini-dry wit, she tells things exactly as they are and does so mercilessly. Required reading for the intelligent disaffected."
PATRICK GALE